For Agatha and Spenser

CHAPTER ONE

Lilliana Wentworth set her basket down on the floor in front of the counter and patted her face on her sleeve. Even at 9:00 AM, the walk from the Rainbow Ranch Retirement Community to Pulaski's Gourmet Grocery had made her perspire. In Arizona, June was the hottest month of the year, the last month before the monsoon rains swept up from Mexico and cooled the air. Of course, then there would be the humidity, which was dreadful on top of one hundred degree temperatures.

Jaclyn Pulaski, owner of the store, was waiting on a woman Lilliana had never seen before. She wondered if the woman, who wasn't quite as tall as herself, was a new resident of the retirement home. Her face was lined and weathered, and her chin-length brown hair streaked with gray was in disarray, strands sticking out from what had not too long ago been a hairstyle professionally done.

"Don'tcha carry any spirits?" the woman brayed. She hooked her thumbs in the belt loops of her jeans and thrust her chest out. "I like a shot of bourbon in the evening, to take the edge off, you know."

The young proprietress shook her head. "I'm sorry, Miss Fordyce. I don't have a liquor license. You'll have to drive into Bisbee if you want to buy alcohol."

"Don't know what this world is coming to when a woman can't get a drink in her home town." Miss Fordyce paused a minute, then gestured at the items on the counter. "Well, ring me up then. I'll have to make do."

Jaclyn proceeded to enter the prices in the cash register and put the items in a paper bag: a pint of Steve's Brooklyn Blackout Cake ice cream, a box of Castleton crackers, and a block of organic cheddar cheese. "Twenty-two dollars and thirty-seven cents, please," she said to the braying woman. After giving Miss Fordyce her change, Jaclyn smiled at Lilliana. "What can I do for you, Mrs. Wentworth?"

Miss Fordyce, who had taken a step toward the door, stopped and looked Lilliana up and down. Lilliana returned the favor. Now that she was able to take a closer look at the woman, Lilliana could see the wrinkles weren't only from the sun. Fordyce had to be close to Lilliana's own age of seventy-four. The red bandanna at her throat didn't quite hide the wattle on her neck, and the bumps of her breasts under her chambray shirt hung lower than a younger woman's would. Not quite to the tucking-in-the-belt stage some elderly women's were, but certainly not as perky as, say, Jaclyn's.

"Oh, I'm sorry," Jaclyn said. "Mrs. Wentworth, this is Fox Fordyce. She recently moved back to Rainbow Ranch. Miss Fordyce, Lilliana Wentworth. She lives in the retirement community."

"Nice to meet you," Lilliana said, and extended her hand.

Fox Fordyce grasped it in a firm grip and gave it a single shake. "You don't look decrepit enough to live at the old folks home."

Lilliana smothered a laugh. While many of the residents were disabled and needed what they now called assisted living arrangements, Lilliana herself was perfectly healthy, except for a little arthritis. All right, maybe more than a little. If it hadn't been for her husband's stroke, she'd probably still be living in their nice little house in Tucson in an older neighborhood near the university. But after the stroke, Lilliana hadn't been able to take care of Charles on her own. She couldn't bear the thought putting him in a facility and going to visit him afternoons and weekends during the time he had left, so had decided an apartment in a retirement community would be a better choice. The ones in Tucson were much more expensive than out here in Rainbow Ranch, and overall, she was pleased with her decision. But she did miss Charles.

"Thank you for saying so," Lilliana said.

"Well, I'd better get this ice cream home before it melts," Fox said. "See you around." With that, she picked up her groceries and swept out of the store, the bell over the door tinkling as she exited.

"She's quite a character, isn't she?" Lilliana said.

Jaclyn laughed out loud. "She sure is. Rainbow Ranch's one and only celebrity."

"Oh?"

"Yes. She was a rodeo queen, a champion barrel racer, up

until not too long ago. She used to practice at Grandpa Ted's ranch after she sold her own."

"Isn't she a little old for barrel racing?"

Jaclyn's gaze grew unfocused, a turning inward while she reviewed memories of the past. "Maybe it was longer ago than I thought. But she did keep racing long after most others her age would have quit." She picked up a copy of the Rainbow Ranch Gazette, the town's weekly newspaper, and pointed to the headline. "Sam even wrote an article about her for the paper."

Of course he had, thought Lilliana. Not much happened in the small town of Rainbow Ranch. Sam Horn had probably been ecstatic to have something to fill several of the six pages he printed every week. Underneath the headline was a black and white photograph of a woman on horseback wearing a white cowboy hat and a sequined shirt edged in fringe. She crouched low over the horse's neck, her right hand raised over the horse's rump, whip in hand, ready to urge her mount to go faster. "I'll have to buy a copy."

"I know she's a bit prickly now, but she really is a nice person." Jaclyn's face softened. "When I was a little girl, she'd spend hours trying to teach me how to ride around the barrels like she did. Great-grandpa was too busy with the cattle back then, and I think she felt sorry for me because I had to spend most of the day by myself."

"Did you ever take part in rodeos?" Lilliana asked.

Jaclyn gave a shake of her head. "Not professionally. I think every kid who grew up on a ranch took part in the kids' events at one time or another, but I didn't have the talent to compete against the real riders. I can ride a horse okay, but it takes a lot of ability to cut around those barrels at top speed." She looked wistful, then shook off the mood and asked, "So, since you obviously didn't come in for this week's paper, what can I get you? A box of Earl Grey tea? Are you out of chocolate?" Jaclyn smiled, thoroughly enjoying her role as purveyor of guilty pleasures.

Lilliana was so glad Jaclyn had reopened the store after her great-grandfather passed away. It appeared that the young woman had inherited Ted's talent for supplying people with just what they needed.

"Not today." She glanced down at the chocolates kept on a shelf in front of the register. A little basket held a half dozen individually wrapped candies labeled Bouchée Noix de Coco and described the dark chocolates as being filled with white chocolate ganache and coconut. Her mouth watered. She tentatively pointed at them. "How much is one of these?"

When Jaclyn named the price, Lilliana was glad she wasn't the kind of woman who was prone to fainting. "I believe I'll take one of the small Godiva assortments instead."

Jaclyn unfolded a paper bag and put the newspaper and chocolate inside it. "Anything else?"

Lilliana, who had heard that Chad Cartwright, the Chief of Police, had asked Jaclyn out on a date, was tempted to inquire about the budding romance, but decided to stick to the reason why she'd come. "I actually came in here today to sell you something."

She bent over, picked up her basket from the floor, and placed it on the counter. Inside sat four of Lilliana's African violets in full bloom. Rich purple flowers clustered around the crown, with beautiful green leaves surrounding them.

"How pretty!"

Lilliana glowed. She'd started to grow African violets as a hobby, something to fill the hours after she'd lost Charles. To her surprise, it turned out she had a talent for raising the plants. She'd even developed one of her own hybrids this past year. But even with exchanging leaves with other members of the African Violet Club at the retirement home to increase the size of her collection, it took money for soil and fertilizer and other supplies. Not to mention the electricity bill from running the grow lights and humidifiers. After she had some success at selling her plants at the spring show, she'd decided to see if she could expand her sales. Only Jaclyn didn't appear to remember the conversation they'd had last week.

For a few seconds, Lilliana wondered if the memory problem wasn't Jaclyn's, but hers. She'd noticed her memory wasn't as sharp as it used to be, but previously her fear was forgetting something that had taken place, not remembering something that hadn't. No, she was certain they had discussed placing some of her plants in the grocery store. "Last week…" she hesitated, waiting to see if Jaclyn remembered, too. "I said I thought I might like to sell some of my African violets, and you…"

"Oh! That's right. I'd completely forgotten."

Lilliana breathed more easily.

Jaclyn turned her head first one way, then the other, her long auburn hair swirling over her shoulders and catching highlights from the overhead fluorescents. "I was going to find a space to display them." She frowned.

Lilliana followed her gaze. There didn't appear to be a spare inch on any of the nearby shelves. She wasn't sure whether she was more disappointed because Jaclyn hadn't found space for her, or because she'd have to carry the heavy basket back up the hill to her apartment.

Suddenly the young woman's face cleared. "Say, I have an idea. Why don't you try Cameron's Flower Shop?"

"A flower shop?" Lilliana visualized the stores on Main Street as she remembered them. There was a hairdresser next to the grocery store, a knitting and needlework store before that, and Cathy's Café on the corner opposite the entrance to the retirement home. Then the hotel, and Mike's Garage, of course, and then you left the village of Rainbow Ranch.

Jaclyn nodded vigorously. "You probably didn't notice, since you didn't go far enough north, but that empty store on the opposite corner has been taken by a couple recently arrived from Scotland. They sell flowers and gifts and things. I bet they'd love to have some of your African violets."

Lilliana wasn't sure about that, but since it was obvious Jaclyn wasn't enthusiastic about stocking her plants, she might as well give them a try. After paying for her purchases, Lilliana picked up her basket and headed out the door to meet these newly-arrived entrepreneurs.

She continued north on Main Street, crossed Canyon Road, and walked the few steps that brought her to the shop on the corner. Jaclyn had been right; she didn't often come this way.

Like most other small towns in America, Rainbow Ranch had been hit hard by the 2008 recession. Small businesses had

had a tough go of it, and many had closed. As long as Lilliana could remember, the corner location had been nothing more than grime-covered windows and a dingy door.

The shop had undergone a transformation since then. The windows sparkled, and the front of the building had been given a fresh coat of dark green paint. Complementing the color were dozens of plants behind the glass, many with brightly colored ribbons tied around the pots. Gold letters spelled out Cameron's Flowers and Gifts toward the top of the window. Just the kind of place that would be able to sell African violets. Resolutely, Lilliana pushed open the door.

A middle-aged woman looked up from where she was watering a rather large ficus. A mass of dirty blonde hair tumbled to her shoulders. Appropriately enough, she wore a loose jacket in a red and green plaid. Her eyes had the crinkled look of a woman who was perpetually smiling. They crinkled even more when she turned her smile on Lilliana. "Walcome," she said "Ma name's Penny Cameron. Is there something I can help ye with?"

Lilliana found the lilting Scottish accent delightful and took an immediately liking to the woman. "Why yes, you can. Have you got a minute to talk with me?"

"Aye. I've always got a minute for a customer." Penny put her watering can down and came over to where Lilliana stood just inside the door. As if noticing it for the first time, she peered down at the plants in Lilliana's basket. "And what have ye got there?"

Lilliana lifted the basket and said, "A few of my African violets. We had a show at the retirement community a few months back, and they proved quite popular. I was thinking perhaps people might like to buy them year round, rather than just in the spring."

Penny looked doubtful. "And how were ye thinking of doing that?"

Lilliana felt the heat in her neck. The warmth spread upward to her cheeks. She was sure she had two bright red spots, darker than any blusher she'd ever used, shining like twin stop lights under her eyes. She glanced around the store. "Jaclyn at the grocery store suggested you might sell them."

"Why would we do that?" A man's gruff voice came from behind her.

She twirled to see a tall man with angry slate blue eyes sending a piercing stare in her direction. He sported a dark auburn mustache and beard and a thick head of hair in the same color. Apparently he'd entered the shop unnoticed while she and Penny had been talking. Lilliana felt the flush in her face deepen. "Well, I thought you might need some plants, being new and all."

"As you can verra well see, we have plenty of plants to sell. What we could use is some paying customers."

"Now, Geoff," Penny began, but he cut her off with a look that could draw blood.

"Maybe I could use something…" Lilliana desperately cast about for something that didn't look too expensive, but might appease the angry Geoff.

His shoulders relaxed just a little.

"We got a delivery of supplies while ye were out," Penny said to him. "Some of the packages were too heavy for me.

Why don't you go in the back and put them away?"

Geoff looked as if he wasn't fooled by Penny's ruse for one minute, but he strode past the women and disappeared through a doorway at the rear of the store.

"I must apologize for me husband's lack of manners," Penny whispered. "It cost most of our savings to come to America and open the shop. He's that worried about not being able to make a go of it."

"What made you leave Scotland?" Lilliana asked.

"I'm not entirely sure. We were doing quite well at one time. Geoff found a recipe for biscuits in a box of things left to him by his granny that claimed to help you lose weight. We made a few batches and gave them to friends. Before we knew it, we had people knocking on our door begging for our biscuits. That's when we started the bakery. Then, a few years ago, something went wrong."

"Oh?"

"People said the biscuits didn't work any more. The shops we had been supplying stopped ordering."

"But couldn't you have tried a different product?" Lilliana asked.

Penny shook her head. "There was only the one recipe. I've never been much of a baker. Geoff certainly isn't." Penny smiled impishly.

Lilliana smiled back at her. The idea of the strapping Geoff Cameron in an apron was amusing. "But why come to America?"

Penny shrugged. "It was just something Geoff insisted on. When I asked why, he said we needed a fresh start. His mum was American, and he was born here, so I guess it seemed natural to him."

"I wish you luck," Lilliana said, then sighed. There weren't many options in the small village of Rainbow Ranch left for her. She didn't think the drug store would be interested in selling plants, particularly with a new competitor having just opened up. "I suppose you won't be taking my African violets with all your troubles."

Penny looked thoughtful for a minute. "You know, I can't buy them outright. But I could take them into the store and see if anyone wants to buy one. I'd pay you something if they sell."

Lilliana cheered up. "On consignment. I'd never thought of that."

"Aye. Consignment," Penny agreed. "What do ye think would be a fair price for one?"

Lilliana raised a hand to her chin and stroked it with a finger. She was happy to find that her skin had returned to its normal temperature. She hadn't thought much about pricing. At the show, she'd sold very few plants in full bloom, and knowing she'd only have that one chance to sell them, she hadn't priced them very high. But even small African violets sold for between five and ten dollars online, and then you had to pay shipping. "Do you think twenty dollars is too much?"

Penny cocked her head. "Aye, it might be. If they were in a pretty pot, I might be able to get that, but they're not. How about fifteen?"

Lilliana hesitated, not wanting to underprice her plants.

"You'd get ten, and I'd keep five for the cost of keeping them up and selling them," Penny said.

Ten dollars a plant sounded like a fortune when Penny put it that way. She'd thought the store owner would want to keep more. "Done."

"Just don't tell Geoff." Penny winked at her.

"I wouldn't dream of it."

Penny lifted the plants out of Lilliana's basket and put three of them on the counter. She headed toward the front window with the fourth. Lilliana thought she might as well look around the shop as long as she was here. She was sure the other residents would ask her about the merchandise as soon as she reported there was a new store in town.

A refrigerated case behind the counter held bouquets in assorted vases: roses, carnations, daisies, just about any flower you could name. Lilliana loved the splashes of color and thought she might bring home a small one to brighten her apartment. But her apartment was filled with African violets, so there was really no reason to buy other flowers.

Displays of houseplants filled several tables at the front of the store. Penny flashed her a smile as she passed by on the way back to retrieve the rest of Lilliana's African violets. She pointedly put the other three on the center table, where they'd be sure to be seen. Lilliana was grateful for the featured position but wondered if they might not better avoid Geoff's eyes—and his wrath—in a more discrete location.

On the wall opposite the sales counter, scented candles and pretty ceramic candle holders filled a large section. Adjoining that was a selection of picture frames and small wall plaques, many reflecting flower-related themes. There were also some figurines in the nature of what one might call collectibles.

Lilliana thought the store might do very well with the residents of Rainbow Ranch Retirement Community, as well as visitors looking for a last minute gift for grandma.

As she browsed around the store, she could only hope that the Camerons would be successful, given the small population of the town. Most residents worked in Bisbee or Benson and probably didn't have a need for the gift items, which they could purchase elsewhere at a much lower cost.

There seemed to be a larger display in the back corner, and Lilliana wasted no time in heading toward it to see what else the store offered. Her delight turned to horror once she saw what it was.

A series of shelves exhibited tiny pieces of furniture, little houses, and even walls and fences. At the center was a large ceramic dish that had been set up as a little scene, complete with live plants and a house. It even had a tiny mailbox next to the house. On the wall behind the display, a brightly lettered sign urged customers to "Take Home a Fairy Garden!"

Lilliana gasped.

Penny, who had finished finding places for Lilliana's African violets and gone back to watering plants, heard her. "What's the matter?"

With a shaking finger, she pointed at the display. "What is this?"

"Why, they're fairy gardens. Didn't you know? Fairy gardens are all the rage."

"They are?" Lilliana hoped her heartbeat wasn't loud enough for Penny to hear.

"Aye, they are. People hope they'll entice the wee folk to visit if they make a pleasant spot in their gardens for them."

Lilliana was thinking she'd have to warn Esmeralda about this new danger. So far, she'd been able to keep the existence of the troop of fairies hidden from the rest of the population of Rainbow Ranch. But an attractive display with green plants and accessories just their size might serve as an irresistible lure to the tiny creatures. Perhaps if she knew where the fairy gardens were, she could pinpoint the places the queen of the fairies needed to keep her troop away from. "Have you sold any?"

"Not yet," Penny said. "But we've only been open a week. Aren't they darling?"

Lilliana had to admit they were enchanting. But she was thrilled to hear not one had been sold. "I think I'd prefer a candle today."

She hurriedly returned to the candle display and selected a small vanilla-scented candle in a jar that wouldn't break her budget. After paying for the item she didn't really need, she thanked Penny once again for allowing her to sell her African violets and headed back to the retirement home.

On her walk back, she agonized over how soon she'd be able to give her warning. It was too hot this afternoon to go hiking. The trip to the fairies' home would have to wait until tomorrow morning. She only hoped she wouldn't be too late.

CHAPTER TWO

Lilliana straightened up with a groan after putting the last of her repotted African violets on the bottom shelf of the middle plant stand. Since it was too hot to do anything outside this time of year, rather than fretting over the latest threat to the secret cave or the cave's biggest secret, she'd decided to put the afternoon to good use. Now that her collection had grown so numerous—largely thanks to turning the second bedroom of her apartment into a plant room and filling it with lighted shelves to hold more plants—there was always some chore to attend to.

When she'd been selecting which plants to sell, Lilliana noticed there were several African violets in her collection that hadn't been repotted in over a year. If she wanted flourishing plants worthy of being judged and shown in the spring, she'd have to be more diligent about repotting. She'd taken this opportunity to seat a few of her hybrids lower in the soil, eliminating the unattractive long necks, and removed spent flowers and damaged leaves from some others.

She rubbed the ache in the small of her back. It appeared as if her arthritis had found a new place to lodge.

Hobbling to the kitchen and thinking of a nice cup of tea, she happened to glance at the clock on the kitchen wall. Tea would have to wait. She'd have to hurry if she wanted dinner in the dining room. As usual, she'd forgotten about eating. She quickly washed her hands and stuck her key in her pocket before heading out the door and down the hall toward the common area.

The dining hall was half-empty by the time Lilliana arrived. Most of the senior citizens ate early, measuring their days by when and what the next meal was. Lilliana didn't have the same obsession with food. She scanned the occupied tables until she spied Nancy.

Locating Nancy wasn't particularly hard. One of those elderly women who was always cold, Nancy frequently wore sweaters, even in the middle of summer. Knitted from patterns she designed herself, Nancy's sweaters gave a whole new definition to the word ugly. The one she was wearing this evening was a multicolored affair. Stripes of blinding red, yellow, neon pink, and turquoise dripped down the length of it, with black yarn used at the neck, bottom, and the ends of the sleeves.

As usual, Nancy was sitting with some of their mutual friends: Willie, the retired black police officer; Lenny, a physical fitness advocate; and Sarah and Bob Higgins. Sarah was officially president of the African Violet Club, although all she did was preside at meetings, leaving Lilliana responsible for most of the organizing. Sarah's husband Bob spent his days watching television.

There was also a new woman, or at least, someone Lilliana hadn't met before. She had thin, white hair, and wrinkles draped her face. From her appearance, she must have been significantly older than Lilliana and her friends.

"I thought you were going to miss dinner again," Nancy said as Lilliana pulled out a chair and sat down.

She picked up the menu and was glad she'd decided to eat. The featured main course was chicken and dumplings.

"Good evening, Lily," Lenny said.

No matter how many times she told Lenny her real name, he insisted on calling her Lily.

"Good evening, Lenny. Willie."

Willie touched two fingers to his forehead, a modified salute, in response.

"And who is our new table mate?" Lilliana looked at the woman she'd noted previously.

"This is Rebecca," Nancy said. "She was too ill to come to meals when she arrived here, but she's making wonderful progress now, aren't you Rebecca?"

Rebecca responded with a rheumy cough. "Pneumonia," she said by way of explanation. "It knocked me off my feet, that's for sure. They had to put me in the hospital. Before they'd release me, they told me I could either move in with my son or go into an assisted living facility. The doctor didn't think I could take care of myself any more. Humph."

"Didn't you want to live with your son?" Nancy asked.

Lilliana cringed a little. Obviously, Rebecca didn't want to live with her son. Otherwise she'd be there instead of here. But

Nancy hadn't thought she might be bringing up a painful situation by asking the question. Fortunately, the answer was simple.

"Who wants to live in Connecticut?" Rebecca replied.

There was a pause in the conversation while the waitress came and took Lilliana's order. While some meals were served buffet style, most of the time there was table service. After the waitress left, Nancy leaned over and whispered, "What do you think of our other new resident?"

"Where?" Lilliana asked, glancing around the room. Just as she found him, Nancy bobbed her head twice in his direction.

"Isn't he the most handsome man you've ever seen?" Nancy asked.

Lilliana didn't respond immediately. She was too busy trying to keep her heartbeat under control. The man could only be described as elegantly attractive. Unlike most of the men at Rainbow Ranch, the new resident wore a crisp, white, long-sleeved shirt, a button at the neck undone. His bearing said he would have been more comfortable wearing a jacket and tie to dinner.

While balding on top, his gray hair and mustache were peppered with darker strands reflecting its original color. His eyebrows were still a dark black, and he had laugh lines at the corners of his eyes. Lilliana wondered what color those eyes were.

She cleared her throat. "He looks like a man," she said noncommittally.

Rebecca snorted. "Is that all you can say? He's the best thing I've seen in thirty years."

Lenny looked put out. He was used to being the most attractive man in the community. Most of the men padded around in slippers and sweatpants. They often didn't remember to shave or comb their hair. Compared to them, Lenny, who was extremely fit and dressed in slacks and a golf shirt most days, was a fashion plate. He probably didn't like his new competition.

She glanced at Willie to see what his reaction was. Willie winked at her.

Lilliana quickly looked down at her dinner plate, which the returning waitress had just delivered, and picked up her knife and fork to slice off a bit of chicken. After putting the chicken in her mouth, she concentrated on buttering a biscuit.

"I think I'm going to knit him a sweater," Nancy announced.

That got Lilliana to look up. "Do you think that's wise? Or appropriate?"

"Why not? Everyone can use sweaters. They keep the air conditioning much too high in most of the rooms here."

The waitress returned to clear the empty plates of the early arrivals. "Can I get anyone dessert?" Nancy and Willie ordered the chocolate cake, while Lenny opted for a fruit plate. Sarah shook her head.

"I think Bob and I will go back to our room," Sarah said. "Bob doesn't like to miss the evening news."

The two of them rose to mumbled good-byes, and Lilliana decided to change the topic of conversation. "There's a new shop in town."

That caught Nancy's attention. "Oh? What kind?"

"It says flowers and gifts on the window," Lilliana said.

"They took over that vacant corner store on Main Street. I went inside to see what they have."

"Anything interesting?" Rebecca asked.

"A nice assortment of flowers and plants. They also have candles and little knickknacks and things." She cut a dumpling in half and chewed. It seemed a little gummy to her.

"Did you buy anything?" Nancy asked.

"Just a candle. And the owner, Penny Cameron, agreed to take some of my African violets on consignment."

"Do you think they'd sell some of my sweaters?" Nancy asked.

Lilliana realized telling Nancy about the consignment arrangement had been a mistake. "It's not the kind of thing they carry. They sell plants and little items, not clothing." She hoped Nancy would get the hint. Apparently she had by the frown on her face. "Is there anything on the agenda for tonight?" Lilliana asked.

The retirement home held lots of activities for the residents. While most of them were in the daytime, they regularly showed movies on Wednesday nights, and often had presentations of one sort or another in the evening. Since this was Monday, she wasn't sure if there was anything planned or not.

"I don't remember anything," Willie said. "Then again, I'm not particularly interested in social activities." Sadness washed over his face, and Lilliana was almost sorry she'd asked. The big black man had lost someone very close to him last month and was obviously still in mourning.

"I have to go to bed early tonight," Nancy said. "I don't want to miss the bus to Benson tomorrow."

"Is that tomorrow?" Lilliana asked. Once a month, the retirement community sent a bus into the nearby town of Benson. Its primary destination was the Walmart, but it was also an opportunity to have lunch out at a restaurant other than Cathy's Café, or stop in a bank if you needed to cash a check, or mail a package from the post office. Lilliana thought she could use some underthings. While not of the best quality, at least they'd be new. If she didn't go tomorrow, she'd have to wait a whole month. But what about her mission?

"Lilliana, how could you forget? It's one of the highlights of the week when we get to go to Walmart," Nancy said.

Yes, how *could* she forget? That was the question. Not for the first time, Lilliana worried that she might have something more serious than simple forgetfulness. After seeing Charles' decline, one of her worst fears was losing her mind. So many of the elderly had dementia. "I'm glad you reminded me. I did want to go this month."

"Good. That's settled, then. I'll see you on the bus tomorrow," Nancy said.

CHAPTER THREE

The sun was barely peeking over the horizon when Lilliana took her cup of Earl Grey out on the patio to enjoy the morning. Enjoy might have been too strong a word. Even at six o'clock, the temperature hovered in the eighties, promising another day when it would soar past the century mark. But at least it was tolerable, and Lilliana did get tired of the conditioned air one breathed everywhere in Arizona until the middle of October.

She closed her eyes, wrapped her hands around her mug of tea, and leaned back in her chair. She longed for monsoon season which, while not actually cool, would provide periods of brief relief from the unrelenting sun.

Zzzzt.

What was that?

Zzzzt.

Lilliana waved her hand around her face, thinking to chase away whatever insect had decided to disturb her morning calm.

Zzzzt.

Bother! Forced to open her eyes and track down the pest, Lilliana raised her head and searched the air around her. She saw nothing. Just as she was about to give up on a peaceful morning on her patio and go inside, she noticed something fluttering among the penstemons planted around the edges of her patio. She leaned forward to get a better view, then had to jerk back, spilling tea all over her clothes in the process, as the creature darted out in front of her.

"About time you noticed me," a voice tinkled peevishly as Lilliana patted at her slacks.

Uaine, one of the flower fairies, a lovely little sprite all in pale green from the tips of her toes to the dainty wings on her back, to the long hair that grew on her head, hovered in front of her. Lilliana was overcome with guilt. She knew she should have gone to visit the fairies before this.

Rainbow Ranch had two secrets: a magnificent live cave rivaling Kartchner Caverns, and the fairy troop that lived inside it. The original discoverer of both had died to protect those secrets, leaving only Lilliana and Jaclyn to keep them.

"Why, hello," Lilliana said.

The fairy perched on her knee, a good distance from the damp spot, legs crossed, and smoothed down the handkerchief hem of her gauze skirt. "I am Uaine, a messenger from Esmeralda."

"I remember you, Uaine. What brings you to me this morning?"

"Esmeralda was worried. You haven't been to visit us in a very long time. She wondered if you were ill."

"No, not ill," Lilliana admitted. "I'm sorry I haven't come to visit." She paused, trying to formulate the reason why. She wasn't exactly sure herself. Sometimes she wondered if the fairies were a figment of her imagination. She'd always been a no-nonsense kind of person, and the idea of the mythical creatures being real amazed her. It wasn't as if she could ask anyone else if they believed in fairies. Except Jaclyn, but it wasn't the kind of topic you discussed in public, and she hadn't seen the shopkeeper other than in the store in a very long time. Talking about fairies could lead one to be put in the category of dotty old women, of whom there were certainly plenty at the retirement community. That could lead to being watched, and her activities restricted, which certainly wasn't something Lilliana wanted.

She was also concerned others might notice her trips to the cave. Although well-hidden by the small size of the entrance and a glamour the fairies usually covered it with, hiking off into the mountains wasn't a usual activity for the elderly. While most weren't physically capable of following her, they might take note of her trips and mention them to the staff. That wouldn't do at all.

"Well?" Uaine rose and tapped her foot with impatience. Lilliana had to resist the urge to scratch her knee.

"I promise I'll come tomorrow morning."

"Not now?" the fairy asked.

Lilliana shook her head. "I'm sorry. I have a prior commitment this morning. But there's something I need to speak with Esmeralda about, so I'll be sure to come tomorrow."

The fairy fluttered her wings and rose a few inches above

Lilliana's knee. "All right then. Don't forget. Queen Esmeralda will be expecting you."

"I'll be there."

The fairy flew off toward the desert, and Lilliana hoped none of the other residents would notice the creature. As she turned to go inside and change into fresh clothes, she saw Mary hobbling along the path from the swimming pool toward the back entrance. She had probably been at the water aerobics class. Given the pace at which Mary was able to get around, Lilliana wondered how long she'd been able to see Lilliana's patio. And whether she'd seen the fairy.

* * *

A short time later Lilliana climbed into the van carrying her purse and a cloth shopping bag. Sarah and Bob Higgins were already seated, as was Pieter Joncker, another member of the African Violet Club. Pieter was a portly widower who had come to Arizona from Wisconsin to retire. Like herself, he was mourning the death of a spouse, or so she'd been told, and kept mostly to himself. He'd won third place at the spring show, but Lilliana didn't know much more than that about him.

As Lilliana tried to decide where to sit, she noticed one more person, seated in the last row of the van—the handsome new resident Nancy had pointed out last night. Lilliana's heartbeat stuttered as he smiled at her, and his eyes met hers for an instant. They were dark blue and deep. She quickly unlocked her eyes from his gaze and settled in the seat she stood next to, one behind the middle row, opposite Pieter.

Harlan Taft, a rather unlikeable fellow filled with prejudice and nasty remarks, mounted the steps of the van and picked out a seat in the first row. Before sitting in it, he held up a camera in hands that trembled from Parkinson's and snapped a picture. Probably more fodder for his What's Up Rainbow Ranch Facebook page. Lilliana wasn't sure she liked her picture all over Facebook.

Raul, the new handyman and van chauffeur, backed up the steps with his hand outstretched to help Mary board. She leaned heavily on the railing on the door, then shuffled a couple of steps until she landed heavily next to Harlan, who grimaced. At least he had enough manners not to complain about Mary's choice of seat.

Raul settled himself in the driver's seat and had just reached over to close the door when Rebecca's head appeared and her hand grasped the railing. The woman was out of breath, indicating she'd hurried, maybe even run—if she could run— and smiled as she reached the top step. "Made it!" she announced triumphantly as she paused to catch her breath.

"Please take a seat, señora," Raul said.

Rebecca nodded, then made her way to Lilliana's row. "Mind if I join you?" she asked.

"Not at all."

Rebecca slid in beside her and settled herself as Raul shifted the van into gear. The van pulled out onto Main Street and headed south toward I-10. "I would have sat next to that handsome man in the back if I wasn't running so late. That'll teach me to get ready earlier. I thought Raul would wait longer."

Rebecca seemed a little old for the stranger, but old wasn't the same as dead. Lilliana imagined you were never too old to be attracted to a man. Not that she was speaking for herself.

"The van usually leaves right on time," she said, deciding to ignore the preoccupation with whatever-his-name-was. It didn't work.

"I wonder why such a fine specimen is living in an old folks home. He doesn't appear to need any assisted living. Of course, if he does need a certain kind of assistance, I'd be happy to oblige." Rebecca leered.

Lilliana tried not to sigh and made another attempt to change the topic. Remembering last night's conversation, she asked, "Did you originally come from Connecticut?"

"Me?" Rebecca looked surprised. "No, I grew up in Sierra Vista. My father was in the Army, stationed at Fort Huachuca. Phillip is the one who lives in Connecticut. He took up with an Eastern girl when he went to college. Yale," she said proudly, before her face saddened.

Deducing Phillip was her son's name, Lilliana said, "It must be hard having him so far away."

"Sometimes." Rebecca grew quiet.

Lilliana hadn't chosen a good subject to talk about. Not only had she reminded Rebecca of how far away her son was, she stirred up memories of her own daughter. Anne was farther away than Connecticut. Or closer, depending on how you looked at it. She was either in a cemetery in Tucson, or in Heaven. Lilliana preferred to think of her as being in Heaven. Certainly, after all she'd suffered, she was entitled to an eternal reward.

Lost in her own thoughts, Lilliana didn't realize they'd reached their destination. Raul pulled up in front of the

Walmart entrance and opened the door to the van. "For those who want to do some shopping here, I'll be back in three hours to pick you up. There are some nice restaurants on Fourth Street if you'd like an early lunch, but make sure to be standing in front of the store at noon. I'll be continuing on to the Visitor Center for those who would prefer other activities while we're here."

"What if we don't want to eat in a restaurant?" Sarah Higgins asked, her face scrunched up with worry.

Raul smiled. "Don't worry. I'll have you back before the dining room closes if you want to eat lunch at Rainbow Ranch."

Sarah's frown disappeared. Poor Sarah. Lilliana knew she and Bob didn't have much money. She hoped she'd never come to a time when eating lunch out once in a while would be a hardship.

Lilliana rose to her feet, as did most of the occupants. Walmart was the primary destination for the seniors, both because of the prices and the fact that it had the best variety of any store in town. She was hoping the retirement community would have another trip to Park Place Mall in Tucson soon. She really didn't like shopping in Walmart.

Raul got out first so he could assist those who couldn't make it down the steps without aid. He held out his hand to Mary. It took a few minutes for the slower residents to exit the van, and Lilliana tried to be patient. At last she reached the front, following Rebecca down the aisle. As she turned to descend to the street, she saw Nancy reluctantly rising to her feet and casting a wistful glance at the handsome newcomer, who apparently was going on to the Visitor Center.

Mary was waiting for her at the bottom of the steps.

"I didn't think you shopped at Walmart," Mary said, pushing her walker ahead of her toward the front door.

"I don't," Lilliana said. "But they don't seem to be going to Tucson any time soon, and I have a few things I need to pick up that I can't get in Rainbow Ranch." She walked slower than she usually did so Mary wouldn't have to hurry to catch up.

"I saw you this morning."

Lilliana's chest tightened with concern. Why did Mary feel the need to mention that?

"It looked like you were talking to yourself." Mary giggled. "I do that all the time, but I didn't think you did. Sometimes I think I'm the only one who listens to me."

Lilliana stopped and focused her attention on Mary. "I listen to you."

"Did you listen to yourself this morning?" Mary persisted.

Rather than deny the fact that she was talking to herself, Lilliana said, "Of course. I wanted to remember what I need to buy today, plus the other things I have to do after we get back. Usually I write things down. I like making lists. It keeps things tidy. But I hadn't thought to bring paper or pencil with me when I went outside to drink my morning tea, so I was saying the items out loud."

Mary nodded as if that made perfect sense to her, and Lilliana breathed more easily. They reached the door, and she held it open so Mary could push her walker through. Once inside, Lilliana studied the overhead signs, while Mary headed straight for the grocery section. Finding the department she wanted, Lilliana headed toward it to choose some new underthings.

It didn't take her long to make her selections, and soon after Lilliana took the plastic bag from the cashier and put it inside her shopping bag. She walked out the door and stopped. What was she going to do for the two-and-a-half hours until the van returned to the retirement community?

CHAPTER FOUR

Since it was still relatively early in the day, the summer heat wasn't overly oppressive. Perhaps she'd walk down the street to the Visitor Center and explore the town on her way.

West Fourth Street turned out to be less intriguing than she'd expected. Unlike the village of Rainbow Ranch, where all the shops were clustered together on two blocks, what she'd assumed was the main street of Benson had plenty of empty space between establishments. It also had plenty of traffic, making her wonder if the primary activity in the town consisted of getting out of it.

That wasn't a very kind thought, she chided herself. But she had grown accustomed to the friendly small town atmosphere of Rainbow Ranch.

As promised by Raul, it didn't take too long for her to reach a series of restaurants: a steakhouse, two featuring Mexican food, a family style restaurant. Breakfast was only a few hours in the past, and it was much too early for lunch. With Lilliana's usual lack of interest in food, the restaurants held no attraction for her.

Next was a strip mall with the usual complement of stores: Starbucks, Ace Hardware, Dollar General. Lilliana was beginning to wonder if the walk had been such a good idea after all. Blaring automobile horns made her jump. Up ahead, two vehicles vied for the same parking space.

Small houses, some of which had been turned into businesses, lined the road. A used book store in one of the former residences looked interesting, but when Lilliana tried to open the door, it was locked. She peered in a window, but the store was dark and showed no signs of opening soon.

A tractor-trailer roared by on the road to her left. Not exactly the kind of peaceful stroll Lilliana had envisioned when she started her walk. When an Amtrak train trumpeting its horn rumbled by on the tracks on the other side of the street, Lilliana decided to duck down a side street in search of some peace and quiet.

While she could still hear the traffic and the trains, Fifth Street did prove to be slightly quieter. Like Fourth Street, a mixture of older small homes and businesses lined the street. She had no interest in the coin-operated laundry or the thrift store or the building supply. Lilliana sighed. Sometimes when you went exploring, you found nothing. This appeared to be one of those times. She should have gone into one of the restaurants, ordered a glass of iced tea, and read a book. She always carried a book, just in case.

She'd continue on her way until she reached the next cross street, then head back toward Fourth Street and look for the Visitor Center. She'd get there early, but surely the Visitor

Center would have a chair or a bench where she could sit down and read.

When she reached the intersection, however, what looked like just another house had a sign over the door that read "Wonders of the West Art Gallery." A slate board propped by the door had the words "Gallery Open" and "Paintings of Stephen Henderson" written on it in chalk. Just the thing, she thought.

A bell tinkled as she entered, and a middle-aged woman looked up from behind a counter to the left of the door. She'd been arranging pieces of copper and silver jewelry in the display case. "Welcome to Wonders of the West," she said. "Have you been here before?"

Lilliana shook her head. "This is my first visit."

"Glad to have you." She handed Lilliana a sheet of paper that had been printed on an ink jet printer. "We have two galleries. This one has some of our smaller items. If you go through the archway over there"—she waved toward the opposite side of the room—"you'll see the larger paintings. We're featuring the well-known artist Stephen Henderson this month."

"Thank you. I'll look around." She hadn't heard of Stephen Henderson, but then she didn't know many local artists in this part of Arizona. When she'd lived in Tucson, she'd often stopped in the galleries near the university or up in the Catalina Foothills to browse.

"If you have any questions, just ask."

Lilliana took her time browsing through the first gallery, but it didn't take her more than ten minutes to see everything in it.

There were some de Grazia prints and some small drawings and oil paintings by what she assumed were local artists. She passed through the arch to see if the featured exhibit held anything of interest.

And almost ran into the handsome new resident of the Rainbow Ranch Retirement Community.

"Pardon me," he said, rolling the r in a softer version of the accent the Camerons used. There appeared to be a Scottish invasion occurring in southern Arizona.

Lilliana untied her tongue enough to say, "Sorry" and went to pass by him for a look at the paintings.

"I don't believe we've met," he said. His voice was a rich baritone. "I'm Christopher MacAlistair."

"Lilliana Wentworth." She paused. "Nice to meet you."

"Nice to meet you, too. Do enjoy the paintings."

"I will." Could she not put more than two words together? Fortunately, MacAlastair continued on his way to the other room, leaving her time to gather her thoughts while she stared at the first painting mounted inside this room.

But she didn't pay much attention since she could overhear the voices coming from the front of the gallery.

"I'd like to buy the picture of the cowgirl," MacAlastair said.

"You do realize that's a print?" the gallery owner asked. "The original oil was sold years ago. The artist had a limited print run made for those who want a copy. I'd be happy to sell you one of those, if you'd like."

"I would."

Lilliana noticed he didn't ask the price. Limited edition prints could be expensive. Was he wealthy? That would be a change from most of the residents of the retirement community.

"Would you like it matted? I can do that for you while you wait."

There was a small pause in the conversation. Lilliana assumed he was deciding about adding the extra cost. Perhaps he wasn't wealthy after all. She studied the picture in front of her. This one was an original oil, and the price tag beside it seemed to confirm her suspicions about the cost of the print. A cowboy was roping a steer at La Fiesta de los Vaqueros, the annual rodeo in Tucson. You could see the tension in his thighs and arms as he pulled back on the rope. A cowboy hat shaded his face, adding an interesting contrast to the lower half lit by the sun.

"I think I would like the matting," MacAlistair said, "if it won't take too long."

"I can get that done for you in a jiffy. Will that be cash or credit?"

There was no verbal answer to that question, and Lilliana could visualize him handing the gallery owner his credit card. She doubted if anyone, even a wealthy person, would carry enough cash to pay for a limited edition print.

She moved on to the next painting, which looked like a battle scene between cowboys and Indians. Lilliana thought the Indians must be Apaches, and the battle somewhere more to the north since the Indians of southern Arizona tended to be peaceful. But it probably sold well to tourists who didn't know the area.

"A little violent for my taste."

Lilliana started. She hadn't heard him come back into the

room. "I'm sure it's popular, though. People do like cowboys and Indians."

"I suppose they do," MacAlistair said. "I prefer cowgirls." He gestured toward a picture on the end wall.

"Oh," Lilliana said. "That's the picture that was on the front page of the Rainbow Ranch Gazette."

MacAlistair looked questioningly at her, indicating he hadn't seen the paper.

"The barrel racer is Fox Fordyce, a local resident who just moved back to town. Sam Horn—he's the editor of the Gazette—did a full page story on her. Apparently she was quite famous in her day." After not being able to think of anything to say, Lilliana wondered if she was now babbling.

"Verry interesting. And how would you know all of that?"

"I met her in town. She was shopping at Pulaski's Gourmet Grocery when I was there." She paused for breath. "Have you been to Pulaski's?"

"Not as of yet. Do you happen to know if they carry haggis?"

It took a minute for Lilliana to realize he was joking. She liked the way his eyes crinkled up when he smiled. From what she'd heard, haggis was an acquired taste. "You could ask. I know Jaclyn does order some foods from Scotland."

He raised his eyebrows. "In that case, I'll definitely have to have a look."

And now Lilliana had run out of words again. She'd move on to another painting, but she didn't want MacAlistair to think she was walking away from him. Fortunately, he rescued her.

"Have you seen the bull rider yet?" He gestured toward the

opposite wall.

"No, I haven't." Lilliana followed his gesture and saw another picture from the rodeo. She stepped closer, the better to be able to examine it.

MacAlistair followed her. She could feel his presence just behind her. His voice was intimate as he spoke. "I've always liked stories of the American west."

"Is that why you came to Arizona?" she asked. Her voice sounded breathless, even to her.

"That's part of it."

He didn't appear inclined to elaborate, and Lilliana didn't want to pry. "These paintings really are quite good. I couldn't help but overhear you buying the print."

MacAlistair nodded. "I can use a little decorating in my casita. I think that's what the woman who rented it called it, a casita. Is that right?"

Lilliana nodded. She'd been correct in her assumption about his finances. The casitas were townhouses, more expensive than the apartments at Rainbow Ranch.

"What brought you to Arizona?" he asked.

"How did you know I wasn't born here?" She'd stopped looking at the paintings and was looking at him.

His eyes gazed back at her, focused on her in a way that seemed to look inside her soul. "Your accent. You sound more like New England than California."

"I thought I'd lost most of my Boston accent years ago. I've been in Arizona for over thirty years." She pulled away from that gaze and wondered why she hadn't said "we" or "Charles." Most of the time, she still included her husband in conversations about the past, even though he'd been gone for over a year.

"Not entirely."

The gallery owner stepped into the room. "Your print is ready, Mr. MacAlistair."

Lilliana assumed he'd go right up front to pick it up, but instead he said, "I'll be there in a minute or two."

His voice drew Lilliana's eyes back to his face. "Are you ready to leave, or would you like to spend some more time here?"

Her heartbeat quickened. "I think I've seen enough."

As the gallery owner handed over the package wrapped in brown paper and string to MacAlistair, Lilliana said wistfully, "I wish I could afford one of these paintings for my apartment."

"You can," the gallery owner said. "Although it will be a bit smaller." She reached toward the shelf behind her and pulled a calendar off the stack sitting there. "We have calendars made up of Mr. Henderson's work. There are twelve of his paintings, including two that aren't on display here."

"How much?" Lilliana asked, always mindful of her expenses.

"Fifteen dollars."

When she hesitated, MacAlistair said, "I'd be happy to buy one for you."

"Oh, no, that's not necessary," she hurried to say. She opened her purse and fished out her wallet. "I'll take one."

"Are you hungry, Lilliana?" MacAlistair asked as they emerged onto Fifth Street.

"I'm going to eat in the dining room when we get back, Mr.

MacAlistair." Which she had planned on doing, but if there had been any doubt, his invitation had cemented her decision. After his offer to buy the calendar for her, she was afraid he would attempt to buy her lunch. She wasn't sure she wanted to start down that path.

"Christopher."

"What?" Preoccupied with her own thoughts, she wasn't quite sure what he was referring to.

"You called me 'Mr. MacAlistair.' There's surely no need to be so formal. Call me Christopher."

"Oh, of course… Christopher." She kept her eyes on the sidewalk.

"Unfortunately, my appetite is demanding I eat sooner than that," Christopher said. "I'll see you later."

"Yes, of course," Lilliana said. She watched as he headed off at a brisk pace toward Fourth Street. Was he escaping her? Did he feel insulted that she'd turned down his invitation to lunch? She hoped not. It wasn't personal. Well, maybe it was. She wasn't sure she was ready for a new relationship yet. Or maybe she was jumping to conclusions.

She made her way to the Visitor Center and browsed the rack of brochures and the small display of merchandise for sale, most of which featured a bat with outstretched wings. When she inquired as to the reason, she was told it was because of Kartchner Caverns, which, for a large part of the year, served as a home and nursery to a colony of bats. She was glad the cave in Rainbow Ranch didn't have bats. At least, she'd never seen one there.

After a while, she found a bench to sit on and took her book out of her purse. She was currently reading one of the Lucas Davenport novels by John Sanford.

She heard the van pull up outside and gathered her things. Mr. MacAlistair—Christopher—was mounting the steps as she emerged from the Visitor Center. She followed him and paused at the front of the van. Nancy had taken a seat in the last row and looked grumpy when Christopher sat in the one opposite her instead of beside her. Lilliana decided to take the safe path and joined Rebecca again.

She and Christopher had been the last ones to board, the others apparently having spent their morning at the Walmart store. Rebecca had a large plastic bag wedged between her knees and the seat in front of her. Once Lilliana was seated, Raul put the van in gear and headed back toward the highway.

"Did you buy anything?" Rebecca asked.

"Why, yes, I did." Lilliana held up her shopping bag before resting it in her lap.

"Anything interesting?"

The woman was certainly nosy, but Lilliana didn't really mind sharing her visit to the art gallery with her. "As a matter of fact, I found this lovely little art gallery on Fifth Street with an exhibit by a local artist. The prints were rather expensive, but I was able to buy this." She pulled the calendar out of its bag and showed it to Rebecca.

"Hmmph." Rebecca pursed her lips and frowned.

"Don't you like rodeo pictures?" Lilliana asked.

"Rodeos are fine. I don't much like the fact that Fox Fordyce has caused such a stir."

"Why not?" Lilliana thought it was exciting that the rodeo

queen was living in Rainbow Ranch again. She might add some life to the town. And she might be a potential friend as well. At least she was active, not sitting around the pool or the dining room at the retirement home.

"I liked Rainbow Ranch when it was quiet. Now everyone's making such a fuss over that woman. Pretty soon there'll be those TV people from Tucson coming out again. And tourists. Somebody'll probably set up a tour that goes by her house. I don't like all that busyness."

Lilliana doubted it would be quite as bad as Rebecca seemed to think. Yes, Fox Fordyce was a local celebrity and would draw some attention for a while, but she couldn't imagine it would be ongoing.

Rebecca leaned over and lowered her voice. "I even hear she's going to start up some kind of Wild West Show, some kind of fundraiser or something."

"Oh?" That was surprising news. Neither Fox nor Jaclyn had said anything about that when she'd seen them. "Where would she do that?"

Lilliana didn't know of any suitable place in town. The retirement community had been built on the grounds of the nearest ranch, and the town was too small to have any kind of arena or fairgrounds.

"I've heard talk she's going to do it at her old ranch. 'Course, she doesn't own it any more. It belongs to the bank from what I heard. But she wants to lease it for some kind of annual event."

"Where did you hear all that?" Lilliana, never one to gossip, wasn't plugged in to the local news network. She did read the

Rainbow Ranch Gazette each week, but Sam Horn hadn't reported on anything like that. Then she remembered she still hadn't read the latest issue, the one with the photo of Fox Fordyce on the front page. That would have to be one of her priorities when she got back to her apartment.

Meanwhile, Rebecca had pulled her own Walmart bag from the floor and started to open it, obviously hinting that she wanted to show off what she'd bought.

"Did you have a successful shopping day?"

Rebecca launched into an endless tale of her search for a dress to wear, how she tried on every dress in her size in the store, and then… Lilliana tuned her out and wished for a speedy return to Rainbow Ranch.

CHAPTER FIVE

The next morning Lilliana was up and out early, determined to keep her promise to visit Esmeralda. The sun had barely risen, but by the time she reached the secret path, it should be light enough for her to find her way to the cave.

Birdsong filled the air as the other winged creatures in Rainbow Ranch greeted the new day. At the sound of her footsteps, a jackrabbit looked up from the lawn where he was feeding and hopped away. Lilliana was sorry to be an intruder on his breakfast.

It was a beautiful morning, still a little warm, but the air would be cooler once she got to the higher elevation of the cave entrance. She crossed the grounds between the main building and the casitas and cut off to the north to circle the end of the row of townhouses. As she got closer to the entrance of the last one, she heard the notes of a piano. Someone must have their radio turned up loud.

But as she rounded the building, the strains of Beethoven's *Moonlight Sonata* wafted from the open sliding door of the patio, and she realized it wasn't a radio playing. It was a real person. She stood, transfixed by the music. What talented resident of the retirement community lived here? Whoever it was, she vowed she would get to know her. Or him.

Lilliana wasn't really a snob, but so many of the residents were content with game shows or soap operas or gossiping about the other residents when they weren't reminiscing about days long gone. Lilliana herself still looked to the future, to the possibilities that life might hold for her. She read, she enjoyed seeing Shakespeare's plays, listening to classical music, and keeping up with new discoveries in science. She imagined someone who could play like this person would have similar eclectic tastes and would be interesting to talk to.

She was still standing there, not realizing the music had ended, when the screen door slid open with a squeak, and a man stepped out onto the patio. Not just a man. Christopher.

He saw her and smiled. "Good morning, Lilliana."

Slightly embarrassed at having been caught out, she felt the heat rise in her cheeks and had to fight to keep from averting her eyes. "Good morning, Christopher. I didn't realize you played the piano. You're very good."

"Thank you. I'm not as good as I once was, but I hope to practice more often now that I have a somewhat private residence."

The two of them stood there, the day brightening, the birds singing, and a soft breeze with a hint of monsoon moisture caressing their skin and ruffling their hair. It was odd to see Christopher's hair fluttering in the breeze. He was the kind of man who was always well-groomed and carefully dressed. Even though he wore casual clothes—a sport shirt, slacks, and loafers—he still was more elegant than any other man in Rainbow Ranch.

"Would you like to come in?" he asked. "I have a fresh pot of coffee made."

"Thank you, I would." Lilliana didn't mention her beverage of choice was tea. She drank coffee on occasion, but generally found it bitter. But for some reason, she didn't want to risk any impediment to this invitation.

Christopher opened the screen and waited for her to arrive on his patio. She entered, and he followed behind, so close she could smell the scent of his body, the perfume from whatever laundry detergent he used, the soap he'd recently showered with.

She suddenly realized she herself was dressed in worn jeans, her hiking boots, and a stained tee shirt. There'd been no point to putting on good clothes when she was going to have to crawl through mud to get inside the cave. She wondered that Christopher had invited her in looking like this.

A baby grand piano took up most of the corner of the living room to her right. "*If music be the food of love, play on.*" *Now where did that come from? Well, Twelfth Night, of course, but why had she thought of that quote now?*

A comfy-looking leather recliner sat beside the piano, a floor lamp next to the chair providing light for reading. On the opposite wall, a fine mahogany cabinet holding a stereo system —including a turntable—was positioned slightly off-center. And over the cabinet was the print of Fox Fordyce Christopher had purchased yesterday, framed in a dark wood to match the cabinet. Lilliana could only assume he'd had the frame available. She couldn't help but wonder what it had held before.

"It's not much, but it's home," Christopher said. "How do you take your coffee?" He strode past her toward the kitchen, which was visible over the half wall separating it from the combination living-dining area.

"Milk and sugar," Lilliana said. "Light," she added, remembering the bitterness. She took a seat at the small table in the dining area.

Christopher busied himself with filling two mugs— matching, of course—and brought them to the table. "Let me know if you need more milk or sugar."

She took a sip and was surprised at how good the brew tasted. "This is fine."

She noticed Christopher took his black, or, at least, without milk. She hadn't seen whether he put sugar in his cup or not.

"This is a two-bedroom unit, isn't it?" Lilliana said.

Christopher nodded. "I wanted some room after living in small spaces for the past few years. Room not just for me, but for all my things I put in storage." He glanced at the piano. "And I wanted to be able to put some distance between my music and my neighbors."

"Where did you live before?" Lilliana wondered about the small spaces. Had he lived in a studio apartment? Where?

"Various places," he answered vaguely. "After I retired, I decided I wanted to see more of the world. I'd seen Europe, of course, but not much farther than that. I took a trip through Egypt, spent some time in India, and lived in Australia for a couple of years after a brief stop in Japan. I haven't really settled down yet." He smiled.

The smile didn't stop the pang in Lilliana's chest at the thought he might leave Rainbow Ranch before she'd gotten to know him. "So you don't plan on staying?"

He picked up his mug and paused it in front of his lips before finally taking a sip and methodically putting it back on the raffia placemat in front of him. "That all depends."

Lilliana took another sip of her own coffee. It was almost half gone, and she was thinking she might have to change her opinion on coffee. "Depends on what?" She could feel the fear and anticipation of the answer in the beating of her heart.

"Oh, various things." Then he flashed his warm smile at her again. "Such as what kind of people I meet along the way."

If her heart had been thumping before, it now was pounding with the implication of his words.

"What brought you to Rainbow Ranch, if I might ask?" he said.

She told him about Charles and how she'd come to like the community here in the peacefulness of the desert. "It's comfortable here, you know. The people are nice, and it's not a bad place to be if you've got nowhere to go." She bit her lip. She didn't want to sound needy.

Christopher raised his mug to his lips and drained it. "Would you like more coffee?"

Lilliana noticed a clock on the wall and was horrified at how much time had passed. She'd have to hurry if she was going to talk to Esmeralda before breakfast. "No, thank you. I really have to go."

"Would you like to accompany me to breakfast?" His look said the answer mattered to him.

Regretfully, Lilliana said, "I would, but I was on my way for a hike in the desert when I heard your beautiful music. I still want to do that before it gets too hot."

"I can't convince you otherwise?"

"Sorry, no. Perhaps I'll see you at lunch." Before she could change her mind, Lilliana rose from the table and headed for the patio. She could feel Christopher's eyes on her back as she went through the door.

She hurried off into the desert, hoping to get to the cover of the vegetation before anyone else spotted her. The rocky path was barely visible, which reminded her she'd have to vary where she walked if she intended to go this way often. Otherwise, the path would become obvious to anyone heading this way, and a temptation for curious casual walkers. Not that many of the elderly people from the retirement home did much hiking, but Christopher looked as if he was perfectly capable of handling the uneven ground and scaling the incline that led to the cave.

Or Lenny, she quickly added to herself, afraid of what these thoughts of Christopher might mean. Fortunately, Lenny and Nancy's one excursion to try fishing in the pond had proved unfruitful. But there was always the possibility he might go this way again.

She reached a clump of creosote bushes and relaxed once she passed behind them and out of sight. The ground began to rise, and it wasn't long before she reached the muddy pond that was the current termination of the mountain spring. When

Rainbow Ranch had actually been a ranch, the spring cascaded down to the valley where the retirement home now stood. The main building had once been the ranch house, and the surrounding desert the range for a thriving herd of cattle. But Arizona had seen a number of drought years since then, and water wasn't as plentiful as it once was.

Certain she was on the right path, she continued to where the spring lazily entered the pool from the foothills above. She followed the creek through its twists and turnings, and the water became clearer and ran faster the closer she got to its source. Almost there, she told herself once she reached the large ironwood which was one of the landmarks on the way to her destination.

At last she arrived at the beautiful pond filled with crystal clear water. She gaped in amazement at the transformation. When she'd last seen this spot, it had been in the moonlight for the wedding of Queen Esmeralda. In daylight, the full beauty of the place took her breath away. What had been only desert was now a garden. A small grassy meadow formed a half-moon around the near side of the pond, and flowering plants popped up from the edges of the rich soil. Lilliana could only assume the fairies had worked their magic on the land to make this green space appear in the middle of the desert.

She also wondered how wise it had been for them to create this out-of-character oasis so near to civilization. Anyone discovering it would realize it couldn't be natural. She'd have to mention that, too, to Esmeralda when she got there.

Speaking of getting there, the sun was awfully high in the sky. At this rate, it would be lunch time before she got back.

Not that she would have a problem with missing a meal, but people would be curious as to where she'd disappeared to. She'd have to come up with a believable story to tell them.

She followed the spring, which skipped and hopped joyfully down the hillside, until she reached the spot where it disappeared into the side of the mountain. Getting on her knees, she ignored the fact that the opening appeared to be only six inches high and about a foot wide. She knew the fairies put a glamour on the cave entrance to prevent unwanted visitors. The actual entrance was more than large enough to accommodate an elderly woman crawling on her hands and knees.

She knelt and dropped her hands to the ground, feeling her way through the mud into the darkness of the interior. The narrow passage gave her a sense of claustrophobia, but it didn't take too long before the changing air currents and the feel of drier earth under her hands told her she had emerged from the small passage into the larger room beyond. Lilliana got to her feet, brushed her palms on her pants, then pulled the small flashlight she'd brought from her pocket.

Turning on the light, the cave burst forth in all its glory; pink crystals sparkled around her and stalactites and stalagmites glistened with the water dripping over them, which provided the source for new growth. But Lilliana didn't pause to admire the cave formations. She was already running late. Beauty would have to wait for another day.

Instead, she pointed the light toward the floor of the cave, disclosing a line of footprints leading to the far wall. Carefully placing her feet in the path of those who had come this way before, she headed toward a fissure she knew existed up ahead.

She ducked her head to pass through the crevice and emerged into a large room where dripping water was the only sound. She threaded her way through a jumble of boulders and formations to continue on the path. The huge room narrowed and the path grew muddy as she approached a trickle of water that crossed it. This was the only dangerous part of the journey. She knew from previous trips that she was now on a narrow ledge. The water plunged over the side into the depths of another room below. It would be all too easy to slip and plunge over the edge, only to be impaled on the stalagmites on the floor of the lower room.

Careful to stay close to the wall, Lilliana edged her way along the path, holding her breath. She let it out when the path widened into yet another room. The large column formed by the merging of a stalactite and a stalagmite at the center of it confirmed she had not taken a wrong turning on her journey. The path circled the formation, and Lilliana followed it to her destination, another narrow gap in the cave wall some thirty yards farther on.

Curtains of white limestone striated with interlacings of red from iron in the water surrounded her, formations reminiscent of strips of bacon. A shield-shaped piece of the same material loomed over a turning in the path. Careful to keep her light pointed downward, Lilliana paused and let her eyes adjust to the dark.

When she opened them, the glow from a niche filled with tiny delicate crystalline formations, helectites, shone just up ahead. She approached the niche carefully and curtseyed.

"Queen Esmeralda."

The tiny fairy—no more than eight inches high—inclined her head in acknowledgement from her seat on a purple silk pillow that covered the top of a small stalagmite. Her pale purple wings slowly swung back and forth. "So good to see you, Lilliana. Are you well?"

"I am. I apologize for not coming to visit you sooner. Somehow the days passed more quickly than I realized. And how are you? And Tam Lin?" she asked, naming the fairy prince Esmeralda had married a month ago. Lilliana had been instrumental in rescuing the prince and his troop from a box of delicacies shipped from Scotland so he could join Esmeralda and her group of fairies here.

Consternation briefly crossed Esmeralda's face, but her smile soon returned. "We are well."

Uaine, who was standing next to the fairy queen, tugged on her sleeve. Esmeralda bent down so the green fairy could whisper in her ear.

"Uaine has told me there is something you're worried about."

Lilliana nodded. "Well, two things now. It might not be wise to leave the beautiful glen where you were married green with grass and flowers blooming. If someone were to see it, they'd know it wasn't natural."

Esmeralda laughed her tinkling fairy laugh. "No need to worry. Only those we wish to see it can. Others see only desert there." Esmeralda leaned forward and cocked her head. "But you said two things. What is the other?"

"There's a new shop in town," Lilliana said. "A couple newly arrived from Scotland owns it. The store sells flowers, plants, and gifts. They also sell something called fairy gardens, miniature bits of furniture and houses you place in a dish with plants."

"Newly arrived, you say? What might their names be?"

"Cameron. Penelope and Geoffrey Cameron."

Esmeralda's eyes widened. "Cameron?"

"Do you know them?" Lilliana asked.

"Not I, but Tam Lin has told me about a couple named Cameron who caused him trouble. They were the reason he was so eager to leave Scotland."

Lilliana's concern escalated. "I hope they're not the same people. But it worries me more now that you've told me that. You see, I'm afraid people in Rainbow Ranch will start setting out fairy gardens around town, and your people will be attracted to them. It wouldn't do for them to be seen." Lilliana paused. "I'm suspicious about the way Geoff Cameron acted. It was almost as if he was purposely setting a trap for you."

"Or Tam Lin," Esmeralda said. The fairy queen cupped her chin in her hand for a moment as she thought. "I think you are right, Lilliana. I shall have to warn my people not to be enticed into resting in one of those gardens."

"I think that would be a good idea." A growl came from Lilliana's stomach, reminding her that if she didn't hurry, she'd miss breakfast. "I need to go now."

"You must not wait so long before visiting us again," Esmeralda said.

"I won't. Please be careful until we know more about the Camerons and their intentions."

"We will be."

Lilliana bowed again and left, wasting no time on exiting the cave and hurrying down the hillside back to the retirement community. By the time she got to her apartment and changed into clean clothes, she had missed breakfast. She settled for a cup of yogurt at her dining table.

CHAPTER SIX

Fox Fordyce pitched the softball in Lilliana's direction so hard, it was past her before she took a swing at it. The ball rattled against the chain link cage behind her.

"You gotta try harder than that," Fox called out and picked up another softball from the cluster at her feet. The two women had come to the elementary school field to test out one another's skills.

On a whim, she had looked up the former rodeo queen's telephone number online—fortunately, she still had a land line —and called her to ask if she'd be interested in forming a softball team. Lilliana's new bat hadn't been broken in yet, and she was eager to start playing again. Unfortunately, in the short span of time since she'd last tried to field a team, those at the retirement home who had once expressed an interest had changed their minds, leaving her no one to play with.

Fox Fordyce had quickly responded she'd love to, and the two women had set a time to meet. Fox went into her windup.

This time, Lilliana was ready. When the ball crossed the

plate, she hit it past her out to center field.

"Yahoo!" Fox yelled. "That's better. Ready for another one?"

Lilliana wiped the sweat from her brow and set her stance for the next pitch. Fox doubled down. The pitch was inside, and Lilliana took a defensive swing at it. The ball hit the bat only a few inches from her hands and bounced toward third base. Fox darted after it as it rolled and turned as if to throw toward first. Then, realizing there was no one standing at first base, she dropped her arm and headed back toward the mound.

The July evening was only tolerable because a slight breeze blew across the field. Next time they'd have to try this in the early morning. Or maybe in October. "One more," Lilliana said.

"Strike three!" Fox yelled as the ball sailed past Lilliana. "My turn."

Lilliana dropped the bat and gathered up the balls lying on the ground behind her while Fox headed toward the outfield to retrieve Lilliana's solid hit. She headed toward the mound, determined to have her own against the formidable Fox Fordyce who, having dropped the ball at the pitcher's position, swaggered toward home plate and picked up the bat.

"Let 'er rip," Fox yelled as she crouched over the plate.

Lilliana sent the ball toward her at the fastest speed she could manage, only to see it returned in a high arc over her head.

"Home run!" Fox pumped her fist.

Lilliana picked up the next ball and felt a great deal of satisfaction when Fox swung and missed. The cowgirl wasn't invincible after all. She bent over and retrieved the third ball, focused on her target, and let it go.

Another "home run." Determined not to be shown up, Lilliana managed two more strikes in succession.

"Another round?" Fox asked.

"I don't think so," Lilliana said. "It's getting too dark to see the ball clearly." And she wanted to quit while she was ahead. Or at least even. "Besides, I should be getting back to the retirement home if I want to get dinner."

"How about we pick up a pizza and eat it at my place?"

Lilliana was surprised, but pleased, at the invitation. "Why, that would be delightful."

Fox cocked her head. "You know, Lilliana, you gotta loosen up if you're going to live in the West. We're not as formal out here as they are where you come from."

"Old habits are hard to break, I guess."

"Where are you from anyway?" Fox asked as they started toward Fox's pickup, a shiny silver GMC Canyon.

"Massachusetts, near Boston," she answered.

"That explains it, then. You probably went to some fancy girls' school or something."

"Well, yes." She was somewhat embarrassed about her privileged background. People usually thought you were arrogant when you went to the kind of private school she'd attended, but she hoped that wasn't the case for her.

"Ever ride a horse?"

Lilliana shook her head, then, realizing Fox wasn't looking at her and probably couldn't see her in the darkening twilight even if she had been, said, "No, I haven't. Horseback riding wasn't part of the curriculum."

Fox snorted. They'd reached the truck and two beeps sounded as Fox unlocked it with her remote entry key. Once inside, Fox started the truck and turned left on Main Street, surprising Lilliana by heading through town rather into the nearby residential section. She'd assumed, like everyone else she'd met so far, the woman lived on one of the streets surrounding the church, but clearly she didn't.

Briefly, she wondered if Fox didn't live in the town of Rainbow Ranch at all, but she turned onto the side street just past Mike's Garage before leaving the city limits. This was an area Lilliana hadn't explored; indeed, she'd never noticed this road before, Starlight Drive from the name on the street sign. Fox swerved into the parking lot of a small building sporting a Mama's Pizza sign. Hidden as it was behind the garage, it was no wonder she hadn't seen it.

"Sausage and peppers okay with you?" Fox asked as she swung the door of the truck open.

"Yes, that would be fine." Lilliana wondered whether she should get out or wait in the truck. Since Fox hadn't said anything, she decided to stay where she was.

Starlight Drive appeared to consist mostly of vacant land. She couldn't see any other businesses or homes on the street. A few minutes later, Fox returned, carrying a flat pizza box. She held the box out to Lilliana, who took it and gingerly rested it on her knees.

"Don't burn yourself," Fox said. "We'll be home in a jiffy."

"Jiffy" was a matter of opinion, but it certainly wasn't too much longer before the two women pulled up into the dirt drive beside a stucco ranch house with a bright turquoise door beneath a portico.

"Home sweet home," Fox said. "Watch your step."

Her hostess pointed to the irregular blocks that created a zigzag path to the door. Lilliana wouldn't want to attempt to traverse the path in the dark. It would be too easy to take a misstep and twist an ankle. Or worse. She followed Fox through the brightly-painted door, holding the pizza box, from which marvelous smells rose, slightly to the side so she could see where she was walking.

A foyer all in tan, from the paint on the walls to the ceramic tiles on the floor, had openings to the left and right. Just inside the entrance, she caught a glimpse of a great room with a fireplace as Fox led the way toward the rear. A door on the opposite side opened into a powder room.

"Put the pizza on the table." Fox gestured toward a dining area at the back of the house. An oak table with four chairs sat in front of a window, and a door beside it led to the outside. The cowgirl halted before an arch leading to a kitchen with bright white appliances. "Then grab a couple of plates from the cabinet down there, if you don't mind." She waved at an area on the other side of the kitchen.

Lilliana deposited the pizza as requested and was opening the cabinet in the indicated area when Fox asked another question.

"Want a beer, Boston?"

Lilliana cringed at yet another nickname. Yes, her name was longer than most, but she didn't like being called Boston or Lily or anything other than her proper name. Fortunately Fox's head was buried inside the refrigerator, so she didn't see Lilliana's grimace.

"No, thank you. Ice water will be fine."

Finally locating the dinner plates, she grabbed two and put them on the table. She was wondering if there was anything else she could do when Fox arrived with a tall glass of ice water and a can of Budweiser in hand.

"Have a seat, Boston." Fox slid into the seat nearest the door and deposited the drinks on the table.

"Boston" took the place opposite. Once they each had a slice of pizza, Fox took a large bite and chewed with enthusiasm, then took a swig from the can of beer. "Just what a body needs after a workout like we had today."

Lilliana took a smaller bite and savored the spiciness of the sausage and peppers. "This pizza really is good. I didn't realize there was a place to get pizza in Rainbow Ranch. You'd think it wouldn't get much business, tucked away off Main Street the way it is."

"Locals know where it is. The people at the hotel can tell visitors, if they're interested," Fox said.

Lilliana finished the crust of her slice and was surprised how quickly she'd eaten.

"Have another," Fox said, tipping her head toward the box.

"I think I will." Now that the worst of her hunger was sated, Lilliana ate more slowly. "This is a nice little house. Do you own it?"

"I do," Fox said. She smothered a burp and grinned. "Excuse me." She grabbed another slice and started eating it with gusto. Pausing to wipe her mouth, she said, "I'll give you the grand tour after we're finished. Shouldn't take more than five minutes."

The cowgirl might be a little raw, but Lilliana found herself liking her. At least she was alive, not sitting and staring at the television all day long. "That would be nice. Have you lived here long?"

"About three months. I was trying to keep a low profile, but then I ran into Sam at the gas station, and he insisted on doing that spread about me."

"What brought you back? There's not a whole lot to do in Rainbow Ranch."

"Don't I know it. You want any more pizza?" Fox's hand was poised on the open lid of the box. When Lilliana shook her head, Fox closed it up. She rose and headed toward the refrigerator with the remains. "It was time to settle down after all my years on the circuit. I tried Las Vegas for a while, then Phoenix, but what I was really hankering for was the peace and quiet of home. Besides, I've got an idea how to liven up this town."

Lilliana followed with the plates. "And what would that be?"

Fox straightened and leaned against the counter. She folded her arms over her chest. "I'm gonna sponsor a Wild West Show. It will give me something to do, and I know enough people who would be willing to come out for a weekend and show their stuff. Why should Tombstone get all the tourist traffic?"

"Why, indeed," Lilliana said. "Where would you have this show?"

"Out to my old ranch, southwest of here. I'm gonna talk to

the bank next week about renting it out for a weekend."

So Rebecca's story had been true. "Do you think they'll do that?"

"Doesn't hurt to ask. Ready to see the house?" Fox didn't wait for her answer, but headed toward the front of the house.

Lilliana took a last sip of her ice water, then followed her across the foyer and into the great room. The first thing she noticed was the painting over the fireplace at the end of the room. "Oh!"

She strode over to it and discovered her first impression was correct. The painting was the original oil of the barrel racer print from the gallery. "I saw this just yesterday at an art gallery in Benson."

Fox nodded. "Steve did that a number of years ago. Gave me the original as a present for my fiftieth birthday."

"It's a lovely painting. The artist does good work. One of the residents of the retirement home bought a print and had it matted."

"Not you?" Fox asked.

"No, not me, unfortunately," Lilliana said. "This is a lovely room." She wasn't just saying that to be polite. Unlike the others she'd seen so far, the great room was carpeted. Two leather chairs were positioned in front of the fireplace. The fireplace itself was flanked by two bookcases sparsely populated with knickknacks. *How you could have bookcases with no books?*

A wet bar was to the left and a large window on the wall to the right. Lilliana turned around and saw a sofa covered in a pale yellow print.

"I don't use it much. TV's in the bedroom and I eat in the kitchen."

They did a quick view of the two small bedrooms on the other side of the house, the larger one with a jewelry box, hairbrush, and small television on top of the dresser, and a remote control resting on the nightstand. Obviously Fox's bedroom.

The front bedroom looked like a typical guest bedroom. Sparsely furnished, the bed made neatly. No pictures or books or any personal touches, except on the dresser. Inside a leather valet tray that sat on top of it was a single key.

Fox led the way back to the dining area. She opened the door to the outside Lilliana had noticed earlier and went through. The sky was purpling with the last of the daylight. The evening star hung in a notch between two mountains in the distance. Even as she watched, she saw other stars appear in the night sky. A coyote howled from somewhere off in the desert.

"You do have a beautiful home," Lilliana said. "But doesn't it get lonely all the way out here?"

"Sometimes," Fox admitted. "But most of the time I'm happier by myself. I've tried living with a man, but you can't trust them. Better to be on your own."

Lilliana thought back to the key she'd seen in the second bedroom and wondered who the man had been who had left it behind. A husband? A lover? A son?

It seemed rude to contradict her hostess, but Lilliana still missed Charles. He'd always been trustworthy. He'd also been her best friend. And Christopher seemed like a decent man.

Could he fill the hole she'd felt since her husband's death? Her throat constricted and tears threatened. Before she embarrassed herself with blubbering, she pushed away those thoughts. "I think I'd like to go back to the retirement community now."

"Sure thing," Fox said and turned from staring at the mountains.

CHAPTER SEVEN

Lilliana climbed out of the pool and wrung the water from her long hair, which she'd gathered at the back of her neck with a Scrunchee before going for a swim. When she'd gone in, there had been no one else about, being the middle of the breakfast hour, and she'd had the pool and surrounding area to herself for a while.

She'd swum ten laps, clearing her mind of the fairy problem and whatever was going on with Christopher MacAlistair. If anything. To be honest, the handsome Scotsman was one of the reasons she'd avoided breakfast this morning. The other, of course, was she wasn't hungry. Two large slices of pizza loaded with sausage and peppers last night had lain heavy on her stomach, and a cup of Earl Grey was all she wanted when she woke up this morning.

While she'd been swimming, Nancy had arrived at the pool. She'd claimed one of the lounge chairs and appeared to be knitting another sweater. Several balls of bright-colored yarn clustered around her, and her fingers darted in and out, up and down, as she turned one of them into a row of stitches on her needles.

"Good morning, Nancy." Lilliana picked up her towel from an adjoining lounge chair and dried her face.

"Good morning, Lilliana." Her eyes sparkled mischievously. "You should have come to breakfast this morning."

"Oh?" Lilliana wrapped the towel around her shoulders and settled herself in the chair. She wanted to dry off before going inside to get dressed for the day. Since it was already in the eighties, getting dry would probably take about five minutes.

"That gorgeous man joined us. His name's Christopher." Nancy paused in her knitting, the better to focus on Lilliana's face. "He was asking about you."

She hoped the heat she felt suffusing her cheeks wasn't visible to Nancy. "I wonder why."

"He said something about seeing you yesterday morning when you went on your morning walk and wondered if he'd missed you this morning. Or whether you were ill or anything." Nancy returned to her knitting, her fingers moving furiously.

Lilliana's heart skipped a beat. Not over Christopher. Over the thought that Nancy's attention had been drawn to her hike toward the foothills. She certainly didn't want to remind her there was anything of interest in that direction. "Well, you know I do different things for exercise. It's getting too hot, even early in the morning, for hiking."

Nancy nodded her head. "That's what I told him." She held up a bright green ball of yarn. "What do you think of this color for a man?"

Lilliana arched her eyebrows. "A man?"

It was Nancy's turn to blush. "I'm making Christopher a sweater."

"What a nice gesture," Lilliana said, even as a pang of jealousy pricked her chest. *Why should she be jealous?*

"Lily!" She hadn't heard Lenny approaching them, despite the sound his thongs made as they slapped against his heels.

"Good morning, Leonard," Lilliana said. She noticed Nancy's approving appraisal of Lenny's physique. Other than the thongs, all he wore was a pair of swim trunks. His well-developed chest was bronzed from spending many hours in the sun. The hours on the tennis court had sculpted his leg muscles into well-defined works of art, something like Michaelangelo's David.

She had been hoping Lenny would give up the supplements that helped him look that way after she'd caught him out, but it didn't look as if he had. She supposed it was really none of her business. Still, she worried what ill effects they had on his body. Not the outside, obviously, but the inside.

A group of senior citizens burst through the rear door of the retirement home and headed down the path toward the pool: the Higginses, Willie O'Mara, and some others whose faces Lilliana recognized, but were still unnamed in her experience. Mary and her walker trailed behind.

Her friends headed toward the three already assembled in the lounge chairs, while the others gathered around a round table with an umbrella in the center and began playing a noisy game of cards. So much for the peaceful morning.

After greetings were exchanged, Lenny announced, "I'm going for a swim. Anyone want to join me?"

"Oh, I don't think so," Mary said. Sarah shook her head. Bob Higgins lowered himself carefully into a chair.

Most of the seniors considered the pool a place to sit beside rather than something they would actually get into. Except for the water aerobics class that was held twice a week. That was something weak muscles and sore joints could do, and the retirement home encouraged the residents to do some kind of physical and mental activity every day.

"I can't wait for the fireworks tonight," Mary said.

"Fireworks?" Lilliana asked.

"You know, Lilliana, you really should pay more attention to the announcements they make at breakfast," Nancy said. "Of course, that would mean you would have to go to breakfast." Nancy paused in her knitting to meet Lilliana's eyes. "You're going to waste away to nothing if you keep skipping meals. First dinner last night, then breakfast this morning."

She felt uncomfortable under Nancy's scrutiny. Yes, she should eat more she supposed. But she rarely felt hungry. If the fairies could leave Willie cakes to curb his appetite, perhaps she could ask them for some that stimulated hers. "I had quite enough to eat last night."

Four heads swiveled in her direction, three of them with expressions that were the equivalent of eager puppies with their tongues hanging out. Only Willie displayed simply moderate interest in the topic.

She quickly recapped the softball practice, followed by pizza at Fox Fordyce's house, and hoped they'd move on to some other topic. No such luck.

"What's she really like?" Nancy asked.

Sarah and Mary leaned in to catch every word.

"I enjoyed being with her. She's a little brash, but she's lived an interesting life. And she continues to stay active. She even has an idea to start up some kind of wild west show in the town."

"Where would it be?" Mary asked, a puzzled look on her face.

"She said something about leasing her old ranch. We didn't discuss it in a whole lot of detail," Lilliana said. "But what's this about fireworks?"

"The town is doing a Fourth of July celebration at the elementary school," Nancy explained. "They're going to have hot dogs and hamburgers, and the school band is going to play. After dark, there's going to be a fireworks display."

"And it's all free," Sarah added. "You can pick up tickets for the food at the reception desk. Of course, it's only one hamburger or hot dog, a side dish, and a drink. If you want more, you have to pay for it yourself."

Free was sure to draw a large number of the senior citizens to the celebration.

"It sounds like fun," Lilliana said. She'd totally forgotten today was the Fourth of July. She had just a few other things on her mind.

CHAPTER EIGHT

The scent of charcoal fires and roasting meat drifted across the baseball field as Lilliana and Willie rounded the elementary school building. The swish of her sundress around her legs created a localized breeze in the still-warm evening air. She'd also chosen to wear sandals instead of sneakers and a wide-brimmed hat to shade her face. As promised, the school band was playing a Souza march. The band had set up in the batting cage, and folding chairs for the audience were lined up on the infield on either side of a center aisle.

Some children tossed a Frisbee back and forth behind the chairs, running and jumping and shrieking with delight. Lilliana hoped no one would be hit in the head with it.

Several food trucks selling funnel cakes and Italian ices and other fast food fare ringed the edges of the field. Local merchants displayed their wares on tables. The owner of the hair salon was handing out ten percent off coupons, and Mike of Mike's Garage handed her a flyer advertising a special on oil changes as she walked by. She passed that on to Willie, since without a car she had no need of an oil change.

Willie leaned his walking stick against his shoulder and folded the flyer in quarters before stuffing it in his pocket. "I hope the special runs for a long time," he said. "I haven't driven my car since we took it out in the desert."

"You probably should at least start it up," Lilliana said. Charles had been diligent about keeping their cars in good running order when he'd been alive.

"I do. I said drive, not start." Willie grinned at her, his teeth a brilliant white in his dark face. "Wish I had somewhere to go."

Maybe Willie could take her into Tucson to go shopping. She hadn't thought of that solution. She'd resigned herself to waiting a month or more before going on a real shopping trip. "I might have somewhere for you to go,"

"Just tell me when," Willie said. "I'm getting tired of sitting around. There are only so many cop stories I can read at one time. Now that I have my new hip, I'd like to put it to use."

Lilliana noticed a crowd surrounding the next table. In addition to some townspeople, Rebecca and Frank and Jaclyn Pulaski were peering at the display. Curious as to what was so interesting, Lilliana edged forward and looked over Rebecca's shoulder.

A large dish garden was at the center of the table, filled with small plants and the furnishings and knickknacks from the Camerons' store. Packages of accoutrements lay in rows on either side of the garden. Penny Cameron was holding up one of the little houses and talking to a woman in a red shirt decorated with white stars.

"It's the latest thing. They say if you put a fairy garden in your yard, the wee folk might come to visit you," Penny Cameron said.

Lilliana's heart sank. This was exactly what she'd feared would happen. She was only glad she'd managed to warn Esmeralda before every home in Rainbow Ranch had a fairy garden.

"Isn't it cute?" The woman wearing the shirt with stars said to her companion, another middle-aged woman who was dressed in a tee-shirt sporting an American flag on the front.

"It sure is," said her friend. "How much does one of them cost?"

"That all depends on what you put in it," Penny said. "Today only, I can sell you the components at twenty-five percent off. If you buy twenty dollars worth, I'll also give you a coupon for a free plant that you can redeem at the store tomorrow."

"What do you think, Janet?" the woman in the tee shirt asked.

Janet eyed the display skeptically. "I think I'll pass. But you go ahead. I'll visit your fairy garden and see if you attract any fairies."

"That dish looks awfully heavy." A doubtful look crossed her face.

"I can hold your purchase for you so you don't have to carry it. Just pick it up before the fireworks. Or whenever you decide to leave." Penny Cameron smiled widely and proceeded to suggest just which items would work best for her new customer.

Willie was shaking his head as they walked away. "People will believe anything."

"I know," Lilliana said. "Fairies. What grownup believes in fairies?" She hoped God would forgive her the lie. "Oh, dear."

Lilliana had just spied Biff Buckley, a television reporter who covered the area for a Tucson station, with his cameraman, stationed in front of a grill full of hamburgers. A handsome young man who was attractive to the ladies, Buckley was annoying and persistent when he smelled a story. Gray smoke streamed in the background for a moment, then Buckley turned to the vendor and started asking questions. He was obviously doing a puff piece for the evening news.

"What's the problem?" Willie asked.

"None, I suppose." Lilliana bit her lip. "I don't care for that reporter very much."

"I think he's harmless," Willie said. "Especially if there aren't any murders around."

She knew Willie was joking, but still she wished the picnic hadn't been turned into a media event. She supposed it was inevitable, though. There couldn't be much hard news on a holiday.

Then the reporter's face lit up, and he waved at his cameraman. "Follow me over here, Joey."

Lilliana saw immediately who had drawn his attention. Fox Fordyce, dressed in a fringed shirt, jeans, boots, and cowgirl hat, strode across the field in the direction of the bandstand.

"Miss Fordyce," Buckley called out. "May I have a few words with you?"

Fox had a different attitude toward the reporter than Lilliana did. She flashed him a smile and diverted her route to head in his direction.

"Let's go listen to the band," Lilliana said.

Willie chuckled and followed her as she headed away from the reporter. They passed by a jumping castle, noisy with the sound of the fan and generator that kept it inflated, as well as the happy squeals of the children inside; a section set up for ring toss; and the Frisbee players.

They sat in the next to last row as the band began playing "Stars and Stripes Forever." Lilliana took off her wide-brimmed hat and fanned herself with it. She knew it wasn't a good idea to expose her scalp and fair skin to the strong July sun, but there wasn't even a hint of a breeze, and she desperately needed something to cool her down. They listened to a few more tunes and, at last, the sun started to fade behind the mountains.

After applauding for the third or fourth time, Willie pushed himself up from his chair with his walking stick. "I could use a glass of lemonade," he said. "Can I get you anything?"

"A glass of lemonade would be wonderful. Wait one minute." Lilliana dug in the pocket of her sundress until she found the meal tickets she'd gotten from Beverly, the receptionist at the retirement community. She pulled out the red one labeled DRINK and handed it over to Willie. "Thank you."

She was smoothing her skirt when a man slipped into Willie's vacated seat and said in a soft Scottish burr, "Is this seat taken?"

Her heart pitter-patted. Had Christopher been waiting for Willie to get up? What should she say?

"Are you enjoying the festivities?" he asked.

"Yes, I am," Lilliana answered. "But, you see…"

A motion slightly to her right caught her attention. Willie, carrying two cups of lemonade, smiled and shook his head. He turned and handed one of the cups to Bernadine Meade, another resident of the retirement community, and led her to a seat on the other side of the center aisle.

"See what?" Christopher asked.

"Nothing. Nevermind." She paused to swallow, trying to moisten her throat. "What about you? Are you enjoying yourself?"

"I have been," Christopher said. "I'll think I'll enjoy it more now."

Flustered, Lilliana cast about for another topic of conversation. "Is this awkward for you? I mean, it is a holiday celebrating our independence from Great Britain."

Christopher laughed. "If Robert the Bruce ha' been more canny, Scotland would also be celebrating her independence."

"Oh, of course. Do you really think there's a chance Scotland will vote to break off from England?" As she remembered, the vote had been close last time.

"Probably not. The young ones have shorter memories than we do. They don't have as much appreciation for history."

The band ended another tune, "Yankee Doodle" Lilliana thought, although she hadn't been paying much attention since Christopher sat down next to her, and the leader turned to make an announcement.

"We'll be taking a twenty minute break," he said. "In the meantime, enjoy the games and the food and the merchandise from all of our local vendors."

"Would you like to get something to eat?" Christopher asked.

"Why, yes." Lilliana rose from her chair and followed Christopher toward the food vendors. She started to angle off toward the grill where hotdogs were laid out in rows sizzling in the heat of the fire when Christopher took her elbow.

"I think I'm in the mood for something Southwestern," he said and headed toward a truck serving tacos and burritos with rice and beans.

Embarrassed as she fingered the meal tickets remaining in her pocket, Lilliana stumbled over her words. "I, I, uh, didn't bring any money with me."

"I did," Christopher said, and firmly steered her toward the more expensive Mexican specialties.

She supposed it would be all right to let him buy her a meal just this once. She chose a taco salad, lettuce and tomatoes with refried beans on the bottom of a crisp tortilla shell, with ground beef in a tomato sauce spiced with taco seasoning on top. She was happy the truck also served iced tea.

Christopher ordered a burrito plate with rice and beans and a Coke. When their food was ready, he asked, "Shall we sit at a table?"

A few picnic tables had been set up next to the food truck, and, just as Lilliana was about to protest that all the seats were full, a family rose from one of them. They gathered up their trash, and Christopher smoothly slid onto a bench. Before Lilliana could go around to the other side, a group of teenagers claimed it. She had no choice but to sit next to Christopher.

She busied herself with unwrapping the plastic tableware

from her napkin, then removing the paper from the straw and sticking it into the plastic lid of her iced tea before glancing over at Christopher. She started when she saw his deep blue eyes fixed on her.

"Shall we eat?" he asked.

Lilliana nodded and lifted a forkful of meat to her lips. She chewed slowly and wondered what topic of conversation she could bring up. She still wasn't sure why a man like Christopher chose to live in a retirement community, but she didn't want to appear too nosey on that subject.

"Have you ever been married?" she asked, then realized that question was quite a bit nosier than why he was living in Rainbow Ranch. Would Christopher get the wrong impression from her question? Then a worse thought crossed her mind. *What if it was the right impression?*

She needn't have worried about the topic of conversation. Instead of responding to her question, Christopher regaled her with tales of his travels: riding camels in Egypt, working on a sheep ranch in the Outback in Australia, consulting on an IT project in Japan. Lilliana thought about her own life, so dull in comparison. She and Charles had lived quietly. She went to her job at a branch of the Boston Public Library—and later the Pima County one—every day, Charles taught his English literature classes at the University of Arizona. In the evening, they'd read or attend a concert or a lecture or sometimes a movie. Vacations had been to London or Paris or Rome. Charles went off to do research while Lilliana sought out museums and gardens. It was much like their life at home, except they did it in another country.

"Do you have any children?" Christopher asked, shocking her out of her reverie.

Even after twenty years, Lilliana's eyes grew moist, and she quickly reached for the tissue in her pocket. "I did," she whispered through her constricted throat.

Christopher put his hand on hers. "I'm sorry. I didn't mean to bring up a painful subject."

"You couldn't have known."

"You don't have to talk about it. Some day, perhaps when you feel more comfortable with me, you might tell me about it." His voice was consoling, easing her away from the pain.

She was rescued from further awkwardness by a tapping on the microphone that echoed off the school building.

"We're about to begin the evening festivities," the band leader announced. "I hope you've enjoyed the celebration so far. We'd like to do this every year if it's successful." Cheers went up from the crowd. He cleared his throat. "Now will you all rise for the playing of the National Anthem."

The band leader turned and raised his baton. He looked at each section of the band to make sure they were ready, then lifted the baton above his head and gave it a firm stroke downward, signaling the players to commence.

Voices rose around them, and Lilliana joined in with her sweet soprano. She was surprised to hear Christopher singing as well, since he wasn't an American by birth, and she'd thought he probably didn't know the words. But he sang confidently in a rich baritone, not missing a lyric or a note.

When the anthem ended, Christopher asked, "Do you want to go sit up front?"

"I'd just as soon stay here," Lilliana said. "I think we'll have a better view of the fireworks if we're not quite so close."

As if on cue, a rocket whistled into the night sky, then exploded in a burst of red, white, and blue, followed by a chorus of oohs and ahhs from the crowd.

"I'll be right back." Surprisingly, Christopher got up and headed toward the row of portable toilets set up behind the vendor tables at the edge of the field. Lilliana wondered if he had prostate trouble.

For several minutes, explosions came from the platform that had been set up behind the backstop, followed by cascading colors and sparkles. Christopher rejoined her, sitting slightly closer than he had before.

Several of the golden brown fireworks that looked like pine cones spread their trails across the sky; others erupted in a cloud of fireflies dancing overhead. Many, in red and white and even green, trailed streamers against the black backdrop of the night. All too soon, a cluster of pops and booms sent the finale of multiple pyrotechnics into the air, blinding them with a sky full of rainbow flashes.

The crowd burst into applause and whistles. People started stirring, rising from chairs or blankets spread on the ground, gathering up their things, and rounding up children.

Lilliana glanced across the aisle. Willie clutched his walking stick and pushed himself up out of his chair. He glanced at her and raised his eyebrows. He was asking her if she wanted to walk back with him. She moved her head very slightly first to the left, then the right. Her stomach did a little flip flop as Willie grinned at her and started on his way back to the retirement home.

"Have a safe trip home," the conductor announced.

"I walked down this evening," Christopher said. "Would you like to walk back with me, or did you come in a car?"

Lilliana shook her head. "Oh, no. I don't own a car, and I walk into town so often, another trip is nothing major." She hesitated. Through almost the entire fireworks show, she'd been conscious of a full bladder. Too much iced tea, or maybe it was just the length of the celebration. She'd been hoping to wait until she got back to her apartment since she didn't like to use portable toilets, but if she were going to walk with Christopher, perhaps at a slower pace than she would have taken alone, she thought she'd better take care of that need. "If you wouldn't mind waiting a minute, I think I need to use the... uh... facilities." She indicated the row of portable toilets.

"Of course I wouldn't mind. I'll just wait here." Christopher sank back onto the picnic bench.

Lilliana hurried off to her destination. The ten structures had been set up in a line with the doors facing away from the field, probably to give an illusion of privacy. In her experience, you could hear everything that was going on inside of one if you were within five feet of them. But at this point, it didn't matter to her.

She detoured to the end of the row, and turned the corner. The hum of a generator supplying electricity to a small light greeted her, and she was glad she'd be able to see where she was going.

But the first thing she saw brought her to a sharp stop. Nancy Gardner was standing just outside the open door of a portable toilet with a gun in her hand. And the body of Fox Fordyce at her feet.

CHAPTER NINE

"Nancy!" Lilliana said. When would Nancy learn *not* to touch a murder weapon?

The petite woman turned around, a finger crooked in the trigger guard of the pistol. Her face crumpled as if she were on the verge of tears. "Lilliana," she sobbed.

Feeling guilty over having yelled, Lilliana rushed to Nancy's side and put her arm around her. "Everything will be all right," she said, knowing it wasn't and wouldn't be for the foreseeable future.

"What's going on here?" DeeDee, the town secretary, probably with the same aim in mind, had joined them behind the toilets. Horror replaced her confusion as she saw exactly what was going on. "I'll call the chief."

"Put the gun down," Lilliana whispered in Nancy's ear. It was too late to keep her fingerprints from being found on what Lilliana assumed was the murder weapon, but she thought Nancy should avoid being seen with it in her hand. It was an image hard to forget, and Chief Cartwright was liable to jump to what Lilliana thought was an unwarranted conclusion.

Nancy slowly lowered herself and placed the gun beside the rodeo queen's body.

"Is that where you found it?" Lilliana asked.

Nancy nodded.

Much as she didn't want to leave Nancy alone, her bladder was getting insistent about filling—or should that be unfilling—its need. And, if she wasn't mistaken, the first thing Cartwright would do would be to block off the entire area behind crime scene tape. "Wait right here," Lilliana cautioned, then dropped her arm and hurried to the cubicle farthest away.

When she returned, she was able to think much more clearly. In the brief time she'd been absent, the news must have spread. A crowd had formed around Nancy and the victim, kept at bay only by DeeDee's constant repetition of "Keep back!"

A ripple passed from the back of the crowd toward the front as people jostled one another. Eventually the young Chief of Police emerged. Behind him marched Sam Horn, editor and publisher of the Rainbow Ranch Gazette. Just as Chief Cartwright opened his mouth, Biff Buckley and his cameraman came running from the opposite direction. The cameraman turned on a bright spotlight and started taping the scene. He was met with angry cries from those whom he'd blinded.

"Turn that off," Cartwright ordered.

The cameraman followed the order, a disgruntled expression on his face.

"Who was killed?" Buckley asked.

"I'll be answering questions later. At Town Hall. Meanwhile, clear the crime scene." Cartwright turned his attention to the crowd. "That means you, too."

Fortunately, people moved back voluntarily, not leaving, but at least not impinging on any evidence in the immediate area. Since Cartwright was the only cop in town, it wasn't as if he could call for assistance with crowd control.

Satisfied the crime scene would remain clear, the chief approached Nancy and Lilliana and spoke in a soft but authoritative voice. "What happened here, Mrs. Wentworth?"

"I have no idea. I came to use one of the toilets and found Nancy standing over the body."

Cartwright pulled a pad and pen from his pocket and addressed Nancy, who looked as if she was going to burst into tears again. "Can I have your name, ma'am?"

Nancy flinched at the sound of his voice.

"Nancy Gardner," Lilliana volunteered.

The chief flicked a glance in her direction, then tried asking Nancy another question. "Mrs. Gardner. Did you find the body?"

Nancy nodded.

Cartwright peered down at the victim, and Lilliana thought he might be regretting telling Joey to turn off the light. Even in the dim light that remained, she could see the blossom of blood surrounding the bullet hole dead center in Fox Fordyce's chest.

"Who is this anyway?" Cartwright asked.

"Fox Fordyce," Lilliana said.

"Fox Fordyce?" The chief sounded impressed. Apparently even he had seen the article in the Gazette. Giving up on

Nancy, he asked Lilliana, "Any idea what happened? Or who shot her?"

"Not a clue. DeeDee called you as soon as we saw her." She avoided mentioning anything about Nancy being there first. She also avoided mentioning her holding the gun.

Belatedly, Cartwright must have realized that the entire town could be suspects since everyone had been at the Fourth of July celebration, and that many of them had already headed for their homes. "Everyone stay right here until DeeDee gets your name and address," he shouted at the crowd.

"What will I write on, Chief?" DeeDee asked.

Reluctantly, Cartwright handed her his pad and pen. The chief had a pretty good memory. Lilliana could only hope he'd remember whatever he could pry out of Nancy. "Wait right here, Mrs. Gardner." He glanced at Lilliana, questioning with his eyes as to whether she minded remaining behind. She dipped her head to indicate her agreement to stay.

"Sam, can you give me a hand stringing some crime scene tape?" he asked.

The portly older man came forward and asked, "What can I do?"

Cartwright scratched his head. "First, make sure no one comes any closer—especially that Biff Buckley—until I get back with the tape."

"That would be a pleasure." Sam grinned.

The chief took off at a trot toward his police car and returned a few minutes later with the yellow and black tape. "We'll attach the tape to each end of the toilets," he said. "We'll have to figure out some way to anchor it out about there."

Cartwright pointed toward the generator.

As it turned out, they used the generator for one corner of the rectangle. Sam fetched a folding chair from the softball field for the other corner. It wasn't the most secure arrangement, but it was probably the best they could do at the time.

"Just one more minute, Mrs. Gardner." Cartwright took out his cell phone and dialed the central dispatch number, or at least so Lilliana assumed based on his conversation. He requested a crime scene unit to come to Rainbow Ranch from the Sheriff's Department. It would take close to an hour for them to drive up from Bisbee, but there wasn't a choice. Rainbow Ranch was too small to have its own forensics team.

Nancy looked as if she might collapse at any moment. Lilliana's own feet had started to hurt from standing so long. "Chief, do you think we could have a couple of chairs?"

"Sorry. I should have thought of that." Cartwright looked around, trying to locate Sam to have him fetch some chairs, but it wasn't necessary.

"Over here, Constable." Christopher stood just outside the crime scene tape with a folding chair in each hand.

Christopher! She'd forgotten all about him. She couldn't possibly leave Nancy to walk back to the retirement community with him. Would he wait for her? Lilliana followed the chief. After Cartwright took the chairs, she lingered to speak with Christopher. "I don't want to leave Nancy," she said. "You can go back if you want to. It will probably be hours before we're done. I'm sure the chief will give us a ride back."

"I'll stay," Christopher said. "For moral support, if nothing else."

Lilliana breathed easier when he said that. No matter how independent she was, it was still nice to have someone around in times of stress. "Thank you."

She hurried back to where the chief was asking Nancy still more questions. Cartwright loomed over the seated woman from his standing position, and Nancy cowered in response. Lilliana decided to remain standing, which nearly eliminated Cartwright's height advantage over her.

She noticed Sam Horn hovering in the background, absorbing every word of both the questions and the answers. Buckley, still on the wrong side of the crime scene tape, fumed.

"Let's start from the beginning." Chief Cartwright looked exasperated, probably not without reason. Nancy was a nice enough woman, but she had a tendency to ramble and change topics and not be very clear on what she meant. "Tell me what you were doing when you found Ms. Fordyce."

Nancy looked at her, as if she might hold the answer to the policeman's question. Lilliana decided to help. "You were probably coming back here to use the restroom. Isn't that right, Nancy?"

Nancy nodded her head. "The fireworks lasted so long—not that they weren't very pretty—but I didn't expect to have to wait this late before I could tinkle. So, as soon as they were over, I ran back here."

"Was Ms. Fordyce also coming to use the restroom?" the chief asked.

Nancy looked confused. "I guess so. I mean, she was already here. There." Nancy pointed at the body. "Dead, I think."

"She was dead when you got here?" Lilliana asked, wanting to make it clear that Nancy wasn't the killer.

Another nod from Nancy.

"What did you do next?" Cartwright asked. "Did you check for a pulse? Breathing? Touch the body in any way?"

"Oh, no," Nancy said, shaking her head. "I couldn't possibly touch a dead person. I leaned over and picked up the gun."

"What?" The word came out as a shout.

Lilliana cringed.

"I picked up the gun." Again Nancy looked at Lilliana for reassurance.

Noticing the glance, Cartwright questioned Lilliana. "Did you see her do that?"

"Well, no." Lilliana sighed. She supposed she should tell the whole truth, no matter how bad it looked for poor Nancy. "By the time I got here, Mrs. Gardner was already holding the pistol."

"So you'd already shot her." Cartwright said the words quickly. Lilliana thought he was trying to catch Nancy off guard, get her to admit she'd done the killing before she had a chance to think about her response. It almost worked.

Nancy's head moved up, the beginning of a nod, then stopped. "No. I didn't shoot her. Tell him, Lilliana. Tell him I didn't shoot her."

Unfortunately, she could neither confirm nor deny Nancy's statement. "I don't believe Mrs. Gardner shot her." Her statement sounded cautious enough to her. She hadn't lied, but she wondered if the chief would catch the subtle difference she'd made by the way she'd phrased that sentence.

"But you don't know for sure."

He had. Chief Cartwright might be young and lacking in experience, but he wasn't stupid.

"No. But anyone could have followed Ms. Fordyce back here and shot her during the show. There was so much noise from the fireworks, I don't think anyone would have noticed the sound of a gun going off."

"When did you last see her?" Cartwright asked.

"Let me think." She knew when she had first seen the cowgirl, but stopped to see if she could recall seeing her any time after that. "It was early afternoon, I think. She was being interviewed on television."

"She was?" Sam asked.

That was a mistake on his part, because it drew the chief's attention to him. "What are you still doing in here? This is a crime scene. You should be outside the tape."

Sam shrugged. "You never told me to go."

"Well, I'm telling you now."

The newspaperman headed for the side where Buckley stood with his cameraman, most likely assuming the chief would be persuaded into talking to Buckley before he left. As they waited for Sam to move out of earshot, a crime scene unit van trundled across the uneven field and pulled up next to the generator. The driver aimed its headlights toward where they stood.

"Wait right here," the chief told Nancy. He strode over to where two technicians were taking equipment out of a compartment on the side of the truck and spoke to them for a minute before heading back.

Halfway on the return journey, DeeDee hurried up to him and handed him his notebook and pen. "I got all the names I could, Chief, but I'm afraid a lot of the crowd left before I started."

"I expected that," the chief said with a sigh. "Thanks, DeeDee."

"Is it okay for me to leave now? Paul took the kids home already. I'd like to tuck them into bed."

"I suppose. We're going to have a busy day tomorrow. Think you can get in early?"

"Sure thing, Chief. And thanks."

As DeeDee walked away, Lilliana took the opportunity to speak up. "It *is* late, Chief Cartwright. I think I can speak for Nancy as well as myself when I say we're very tired. You're going to have your hands full with the crime scene people for a while. I'm sure Nancy would be willing to come to Town Hall tomorrow and answer any more questions you might have."

Cartwright looked as if he might object, but then reconsidered. "I suppose that would be okay. The two of you can go."

"Come along, Nancy," Lilliana said. "You can walk back to the retirement home with Christopher and me."

Speaking of Christopher, where had he disappeared to? After offering his moral support, she hadn't seen him anywhere nearby.

Nancy looked dismayed as she followed her friend toward the crime scene tape boundary. "I'm too tired to walk now, Lilliana. Do you think someone could give me a ride?"

Sam magically appeared just outside the crime scene tape in

front of them. "I can do it."

"Oh, would you?" Nancy asked.

Lilliana was less sanguine. "Will you promise not to pester her with questions?"

"I have more heart than that, Mrs. Wentworth," Sam said in a wounded tone of voice.

She felt ashamed. Of course he did. Sam was local people, not anything like Biff Buckley. "My apologies, Sam. Thank you."

They ducked under the tape as Sam lifted it to shoulder height for them. There was still no sign of Christopher.

"Can I give you a ride back, too?" Sam asked.

Christopher's baritone boomed as he emerged out of the darkness. "That won't be necessary."

Sam looked him up and down. "And who might you be?"

"Christopher MacAlistair. I recently moved into the Rainbow Ranch Retirement Community."

"You know this gentleman?" Sam asked Lilliana.

"We've become acquainted."

"Be careful," Sam said sotto voce, then turned to Nancy. "Let's go, Mrs. Gardner. My vehicle is parked in front of the school."

"Are you sure you want to walk back?" Christopher asked as Sam and Nancy headed off.

"I'm sure. I think I need the walk to clear my head."

Unfortunately, Lilliana's head refused to empty itself of the image of Fox's body with Nancy standing over it. She kept reliving the scene and thinking about the implications of another murder in the formerly peaceful village of Rainbow

Ranch.

They walked in silence until they reached Main Street. Christopher looked both ways, then took Lilliana's hand before stepping into the street. She had the urge to protest the intimacy, but his touch brought comfort—and a distraction—to her troubled mind.

When they reached the other side, Christopher asked, "Does the officer really think that foolish old woman shot the cowgirl?"

For a moment, Lilliana was jolted by the idea of Nancy being called an old woman. She was several years older than Nancy. If Christopher thought Nancy was old, then what was she? Then she remembered that, although in her mind she was still young, her body told a different story. They were all old. Even Christopher. "I hope not. What would Nancy's motive be?"

"I hope you're not expecting me to help you with that."

Lilliana regarded his face, wondering what he could possibly mean by that remark, only to see his smile and a twinkle in his eye. He was joking. "Only if you know something I don't," she responded in kind.

"Maybe she tried to give her a sweater, and Miss Fordyce wouldn't take it."

"Did Nancy…?"

"Aye," Christopher said. "She told me she was knitting one of those monstrosities for me."

"You didn't…?" Lilliana didn't know how to ask him. Nancy meant well. She couldn't help it if she couldn't cook and her taste in knitting projects was, to say the least, bizarre.

He shook his head. "No, I didn't tell her I wouldn't wear it. Perhaps you could suggest she give the sweater to someone else."

"I'm not sure who I would recommend," Lilliana said as they passed the gazebo.

"Do you want to go inside?" Christopher slowed his steps. "Or should we sit out here for a while longer?" He gestured toward the gazebo.

Lilliana was torn. Although she was tired from being outside for most of the day and the excitement of the evening's events, she wasn't quite ready to leave Christopher's company. "Well, perhaps for a few minutes."

"Good." Christopher led the way up the three steps and sat on the bench inside. She followed, being careful to leave a couple of inches between them when she joined him on the bench.

"Is it always this hot at night?" he asked.

"In July it is. Not in October."

"It's a long way until October. I don't know if I'll even be here then."

"But you just got here," Lilliana protested.

"I told you I'm restless. I might decide to move on. Or I might decide to stay. It all depends on what happens."

She wasn't sure she wanted to pursue what would have to happen for him to stay. "I've become accustomed to Rainbow Ranch. I've made friends, and the town is just big enough to be interesting and small enough so you get to know people. It's comfortable, especially for a woman alone."

"Do you plan on always being alone?" he asked.

Her heart beat a bit faster. "It's not always what one intends," Lilliana said. "Sometimes things happen that you hadn't planned."

"I find it appealing to have someone to share my life with." His voice was softer as he took her hand in his. "I like to travel, but doing it alone isn't always fun. It would be nice to have someone with whom to discuss what you've seen over dinner, see things through their eyes instead of your own."

"I haven't left Arizona in a very long time." Lilliana felt wistful. It would be nice to get out and see more of the world. She'd always wanted to travel. Maybe she'd become *too* comfortable.

"You might want to think about it." His thumb stroked the back of her hand, a gesture that felt more intimate than it actually was.

She looked up to find him gazing at her with affection. She couldn't help but gaze back. He leaned toward her, and she so wanted to respond by leaning toward him in return. But she barely knew him. What was she getting herself into? She pulled her hand from his and got to her feet. "I think it's time to go inside. I'm really quite tired."

His face held a question, and she quickly turned away before her own expression could give him an answer, even though she wasn't sure what that answer would be. He slowly rose beside her. "Let's go in, then."

CHAPTER TEN

The next morning, Lilliana decided she would skip breakfast in the dining room and have tea on her patio. She wasn't avoiding Christopher, she told herself. It was just because she'd eaten so much at the Fourth of July celebration yesterday, she really wasn't hungry.

She knew she was lying.

As she drank her cup of Earl Grey, she went over what she was going to do today. It was almost time for the monthly meeting of the African Violet Club. It didn't appear as if enough residents were interested to grow the membership much, and she thought they might need to encourage some town people to join. Perhaps she'd take a walk and visit the office of the Rainbow Ranch Gazette. Find out how much it would cost to take out a small ad. And perhaps ask Sam if he'd learned anything more about the murder last night after she'd left.

On the way, she might stop by Cameron's Flowers and Gifts and see if any of her African violets had sold.

After lunch, she should try starting more of her Royal Purple African violets. She might as well be optimistic about demand and ramp up her supply. While she was at it, perhaps she should start some of her True Blue hybrid as well. That one had been popular at the show and sale they'd held a few months back.

And, if she didn't see Nancy at lunch, she really should seek her out at dinner. Find out if she'd spoken any further to Chief Cartwright. Remind her to ask for a lawyer if he started accusing her of the murder.

She remembered it was Wednesday and wondered what movie the retirement home was showing tonight. Popcorn and a movie sounded like fun. A musical would be fun, something like *Meet Me in Saint Louis* or *Brigadoon* or…

Why had she thought of *Brigadoon?* Could it have anything to do with Christopher? Or was it just a coincidence? What if he showed up at the movie tonight? What would she do?

She shook her head. Enough! She was acting like a fool. Better to do something productive and get her mind off the handsome Scotsman.

A short time later, Lilliana strolled down the driveway of the Rainbow Ranch Retirement Community, enjoying the fact that it was downhill on this warm morning. Of course, that meant it would be uphill on the return trip. It would also be warmer. Hopefully, she'd accomplish her errands before the heat became unbearable.

She was tempted to stop and talk to Jaclyn on her way to the flower shop, but she had errands to accomplish and reluctantly passed the grocery by.

Cameron's was busy for a Wednesday morning. Perhaps some of the people who had seen the display yesterday at the Fourth of July celebration had decided to come back and make a purchase. Much to her dismay, a young woman stood at the counter, an assortment of the fairy garden components in front of her. Penny Cameron was cheerfully ringing up the items and placing them in a large plastic bag.

At least she had been able to warn Esmeralda. Hopefully the fairies would stay away from the new temptation.

A couple browsed in the aisle of houseplants, while an older woman scrutinized the display of knickknacks. Lilliana had seen her African violet still in the shop window, but that was to be expected. She assumed that plant would be the last to be sold, since its purpose was to attract buyers into the store. But disappointment flooded over her when she saw that all of her plants were still there. Not a one had been sold.

She turned to leave the store and almost ran into Penny. "Good morning."

"I saw you counting the plants," Penny said. "Perhaps when more of the buds bloom, customers will be more interested."

"Perhaps."

"You know, they might sell better if each were in a pretty ceramic pot instead of the plain plastic ones. I could sell you some at a discount, and you could repot them."

Lilliana looked where Penny pointed. A nearby fixture held an assortment of pots in different sizes, from small enough to hold seedlings to large enough for a ficus or rubber plant. She particularly looked at the card which had the prices for each size on it. Even at a discount, buying four or five pots—not to mention more for the additional plants she hoped to sell—would be too expensive. The idea had been to earn money, not to spend it.

She shook her head. "Not at this time. Perhaps in a couple of weeks, if you sell some of my African violets."

"It's up to you," Penny said. "Is there anything else I can help you with?" She eyed the woman near the knickknacks, and Lilliana could tell she was anxious about losing a sale.

"Not today. I'll stop by next week."

"Have a nice day," Penny called out as she headed toward the other customer.

Lilliana continued on Main Street, walking slower than she had before she'd entered the flower shop, and not just because of the heat. She had hoped at least one plant would be sold, dreamed of two or even three. She turned onto Canyon Road and, with the turning, her spirits lifted a bit. After all, her violets had been in the shop only a few days. Perhaps the newspaper ad she was going to place would not only bring the African Violet Club some new members, it might encourage some of Rainbow Ranch to inquire about the plants themselves at the flower shop.

Just before she reached the Presbyterian church, a small side street called Camino de la Montaña headed north. On the northwest corner sat Sam Horn's house, with Rainbow Ranch Gazette spelled out on the front window. Sam had turned his living room into the newspaper office after his wife passed away, and shut down the office which used to occupy the building that was now Cameron's Flowers and Gifts. Lilliana didn't bother to knock before she opened the door and entered.

Sam, ever old-fashioned, wore a white dress shirt with his tie loosened and his sleeves rolled up. He sat at an antique roll-top desk making notes on a yellow legal pad.

Lilliana crossed to the wooden counter opposite the door. "Good morning, Sam," she said.

Sam rose from his desk at the sound of her voice. "Good morning, Mrs. Wentworth. What can I do for you this fine day?"

"I'd like to place an ad in the paper."

He stepped over to the counter and reached underneath. "Will that be a display ad or a classified?" he asked as he shoved the paper form toward her.

"Oh, just a classified. Do you happen to have a pen?"

Sam reached under the counter again and rattled around in some container or other before coming up with a pen. "Minimum charge is ten dollars. That covers up to twenty-five words. Five dollars for every twenty-five words after that."

She paused with the pen raised in her hand and counted in her head. She believed she could squeeze all the information about the meeting into twenty-five words if she used them carefully. Once she had her thoughts organized, she printed out the message on the form, filled in her name, address, and telephone number at the bottom, and pushed the form over to Sam.

"Trying to drum up some new customers, I see." Sam counted the words she'd written. "That will be ten dollars."

Lilliana pulled her wallet out of her pocket and took a twenty dollar bill from it.

As Sam counted out the change, he casually asked, "Any news on the murder?"

"None that I know of. But I haven't spoken to Nancy or the chief this morning. I was hoping you might have news for me."

"Cartwright isn't talking. I hung around last night after I dropped Mrs. Gardner off, same as Buckley, but the chief just issued a formal statement of what we already knew. You'll tell me if you hear anything?"

"Of course," Lilliana said, but reserved exactly how much she'd tell the newspaperman depending on what she found out. There was no use having too much information in the weekly paper.

"Anything else going on at the retirement home?" Sam asked hopefully. "Are you having any more softball games?"

It sounded as if Sam was having problems filling column inches. She thought the murder would take up plenty of room, but then she remembered that her game often filled most of the sports page. "No, unfortunately. I think I'm going to have to give up on the idea of having a softball team. I was hoping Fox would help form one in town, but that's not possible now."

"It's Fox, is it?" Sam looked more interested than Lilliana would have liked.

"Uh, it was." She decided there was no point in holding back. "A couple of days ago, I called her and asked if she'd be interested in getting together to hit a ball around. She seemed like one of the few people who not only had time to do it, but was physically fit enough to enjoy it. So we did. We went to the schoolyard and took turns batting."

"Too bad. I kind of enjoyed doing coverage of the games.

Anything else happening?"

"Nothing much." Before she could stop herself, she added, "Unless you want to count Christopher MacAlistair." She laughed. "He's caused quite a stir among the female population." Realizing what she'd said, Lilliana felt a flush rise in her face.

"I would imagine." Sam appraised her, and she wondered if he noticed the blush. "You two seemed pretty friendly last night. Do you know how he came to Rainbow Ranch?"

Lilliana was puzzled. Christopher had been vague on that topic, but Sam seemed to be implying there was something that he knew and she didn't. Not sure she wanted to hear the answer, she asked, "How?"

"He drove into town with our dear, departed rodeo queen. Miss Fordyce told me he was living at her house up until about a month ago." Sam paused as if wondering whether to keep talking or not.

Lilliana's heart had risen to her throat. The key in the valet tray must have been Christopher's. She didn't dare say much more, but managed to squeak out, "Oh?"

"I think they had some kind of falling out," Sam said.

Lilliana swallowed. "Any idea over what?"

"I didn't get the whole story. She didn't want to talk about it, and I was more interested in her than him. Jaclyn Pulaski might know."

"Jaclyn?" For the second time today, Lilliana wondered if she should stop in at Pulaski's Gourmet Grocery. *Did she want to?*

Better to find out sooner rather than later. If MacAlistair

was some kind of Lothario, she'd be better off to steer clear of him. She was feeling better about cutting their conversation short last night. If he wasn't a Casanova, there was always the chance he was on the rebound. You never wanted to start a relationship with someone on the rebound in Lilliana's experience. Not that she had all that much. Experience, that is. She'd met Charles while she was studying at Simmons and hadn't been interested in anyone else since. Well, there had been Ted, but she hadn't known him long enough for a relationship to develop.

"Lilliana?" Sam asked.

She tore herself away from her inner musings. "So the ad will appear in this week's paper?"

"Yes. Anything else I can do for you?"

"No. No, thank you." She hurried out of the newspaper office.

On the walk home, she wondered if you ever got over the ups and downs of romance. You would think that, in time, you'd learn not to be hurt so easily. But apparently not. What was it they used to say? Something about playing for bigger stakes?

CHAPTER ELEVEN

The population in the dining room was sparse when Lilliana entered. Having skipped breakfast, she'd gone down as soon as they were open for lunch. Even though she was early, Nancy and Rebecca were earlier. Their plates of chicken parmesan with spaghetti were half eaten when Lilliana joined them.

"We missed you at breakfast," Nancy said. "Did you sleep late?"

Lilliana decided to tell a half truth. "Why, yes. It was a late night last night. Have you heard any more from the Chief?"

A worried look crossed Nancy's face. "He wants me to come to the police station this afternoon and give a formal statement. What's a formal statement?"

"All he means is that he wants what you know in writing," Lilliana tried to sound reassuring. "You'll need to remember the details of what happened last night."

"What if I don't remember?"

"Make it up," Rebecca said as she jabbed a piece of chicken.

"I don't think that's a good idea," Lilliana said. "When

dealing with the police, it's better to tell the truth. They have ways of figuring out if you lie."

She looked around the dining room, trying to spot a server to give her order to. A young woman noticed her and hurried over. The chicken parmesan looked good, so she ordered that.

Willie's walking stick thumped across the floor as he made his way toward them. "May I join you ladies?"

"Of course," Lilliana said.

Willie took a seat and also ordered the chicken parmesan.

"I'd like it better if that handsome new man joined us." Rebecca grinned wickedly.

"I think he's too young for you," Nancy said pointedly.

Fortunately, Christopher was nowhere to be seen. If he'd joined them at the table, it would be not a love triangle, but a quadrangle. Assuming she herself was still interested in him, which she wasn't entirely certain she was. "Do you want me to come with you?"

Both Nancy and Rebecca's heads swiveled in her direction, neither of them looking like they comprehended what she was talking about.

"To Town Hall," she elaborated. "To meet with Chief Cartwright."

Understanding followed by gratitude washed over Nancy's face. "Oh, would you, Lilliana?"

"Of course."

"I told him I'd be there at two. I'd better go change my clothes now."

She thought Nancy looked perfectly fine, but if changing into something more formal would make her feel better—and use up the time until two o'clock—it wouldn't be a bad thing. "I'll knock on your door at one-thirty," Lilliana said.

"Thank you for offering." Nancy rose and hurried out of the dining room.

The server brought the lunch plates for Lilliana and Willie, and they turned their attention to their food. Rebecca was quiet for a few minutes, then as if she needed to fill the void, spoke up. "You know, I wasn't joking about Nancy making things up."

Willie stopped twirling spaghetti around his fork and looked up from his plate. "About what?"

Lilliana filled him in on the chief's request and Nancy's concern about remembering details. Then she turned back to Rebecca. "What are you talking about?"

"I was sitting with her last night, watching the fireworks, you know. We were wondering where Mr. MacAlistair had disappeared to—we'd both seen him earlier in the day, but lost track of him—and commenting on how Fox Fordyce had been eying him when she showed up."

Lilliana's head hurt. Had anyone seen her and Christopher together? What had Fox thought of Lilliana eating at the picnic table with her ex-boyfriend? If that's what he was. What kind of relationship had they had? Why had they broken up? It was obvious Christopher had moved into the retirement community after the breakup. Had he decided on staying there with hopes of getting back together?

"Nancy was curious as to why Fox Fordyce was so interested in MacAlistair. So, when the cowgirl headed toward the portable toilets, Nancy said she was going to follow her and see if Christopher was there.

"She got up right away and ran after her. Left me all by myself." Rebecca frowned.

So Nancy hadn't accidentally discovered Fox's body. If she'd followed the woman, she must have seen who shot her. Was it possible Nancy really was the murderer? "Are you sure?"

"Am I sure? I was sitting right there, wasn't I?" Rebecca looked insulted. She rose from her chair, her face set in an angry scowl, and stormed off, muttering to herself. "I don't have to take that kind of treatment. Call me a liar, will she?"

Lilliana and Willie stared after her until she went through the doors of the dining room. Willie shook his head. "I'll never understand women."

Lilliana wasn't sure she would, either. Especially all the elderly ones at the retirement home. "I'm worried about Nancy."

"I understand." Willie sopped up the sauce on his plate with a piece of Italian bread slathered in butter. He'd eaten everything else, which surprised Lilliana.

When the fairies had found out he needed to lose weight, they'd started leaving him a wafer every morning that decreased his appetite. Although he'd gotten through the hip surgery, he'd told her he intended to get back in shape now that he was more mobile. He hadn't finished a meal in weeks. Now he'd not only finished all the food on his plate, he was eying the spaghetti and sauce she hadn't eaten.

"Are you going to eat that?" he finally asked.

She pushed her plate toward him. "No, you can have it. Aren't you getting a wafer every morning any more?"

Willie dug into the spaghetti with relish, chewed and swallowed before answering. "Oh, I am, but lately they've tasted like something that came out of the back end of a horse. I've been throwing them out."

Lilliana filed that away in her memory. Were the wafers really different or was Willie using the taste as an excuse? "Would you mind if I tasted one?"

"I don't think you want to."

"Nevertheless, I'd like to see for myself."

"Fine. I'll bring the one I get tomorrow to breakfast."

"Now, don't you get all in a huff."

"Sorry," Willie said shamefacedly. "I'm disappointed in myself, is all. I thought I could lose more weight without the wafers, but I get so hungry."

"There might be something I can do about that."

"Like what?"

Lilliana wasn't about to tell Willie about the fairies. She had a suspicion one of the tricksy ones had decided to use magic not to help Willie lose weight, but to gain it back. Ignoring his question, she said, "I can't imagine Nancy would shoot anyone, but Rebecca's story sounds incriminating."

"I'm with you on that one. Mrs. Gardner is a sweet old lady. Her taste in sweaters is a little odd, and her idea of cooking is pretty bad, but I think she's harmless."

"I'm afraid she's going to get herself into trouble." Lilliana tapped her fingers on the table.

"I know that look," Willie said. "You're thinking of trying to solve this case, aren't you?"

"Yes, I am. Would you be willing to help me again?"

Willie had retired from the Tucson Police Department when his hip gave out. He'd been Captain of the Major Crimes Division and, coincidentally, Chad Cartwright's boss. His experience had been invaluable in solving the two previous murders in Rainbow Ranch. While Lilliana was fairly competent in putting clues together, Willie O'Mara had the professional expertise to interpret the evidence. And to know how to talk to the young police chief in language he'd understand.

"I might be able to do that," Willie said. "It was getting too quiet around here anyway."

Lilliana smiled. "Good."

CHAPTER TWELVE

"The door's locked." Nancy gripped the handle on the passenger's side of Willie's 2005 Lincoln Town Car as Lilliana pressed the button several times.

"Stop pulling on the handle for a minute," Lilliana said, trying to keep the exasperation out of her voice. Once more, she pressed the button to unlock the car doors. This time she heard the click of the locks disengaging. "Now try it."

Nancy smiled with relief as she opened the car door and got out. Lilliana waited until Nancy had closed it again, then got out herself and locked the car. When the thermometer on her patio read 110 degrees, she had decided to borrow Willie's car rather than attempting the walk from the retirement home to Town Hall. Even if she could have made it, she was fairly sure Nancy wouldn't have been able to.

The July sun baked the black asphalt in the rear parking lot, so hot Lilliana could feel the heat through the soles of her shoes. "Let's get inside before we melt."

She hurried across the paving to the rear entrance of the

building and climbed the steps to the door. Nancy followed. She'd never come in this door and was afraid it might be locked, but fortunately it yielded to her touch and opened.

The hallway, even though lit by overhead fluorescents, seemed dim after the bright sunshine outside. Lilliana led the way to the lobby.

"Good afternoon, Mrs. Wentworth," DeeDee said from the reception desk, then spotted Nancy as she caught up. "Good morning, Mrs. Gardner. What can I do for you?"

"We're here to see the chief," Lilliana told her.

"Let me tell him you're here," DeeDee said. She picked up the phone and relayed the information.

A few moments later, Chief Cartwright opened the door to his office and waved them in.

"Thanks for coming down this afternoon," he said. "Hot enough for you?"

"Awful," Nancy said. Her face was the color of a stoplight under her platinum blonde hair, and drops of perspiration covered her skin.

Lilliana noticed Nancy was wearing one of her colorful sweaters. "You might want to take your sweater off."

"Let me get you some water," the chief said. He picked up the phone, and a few moments later DeeDee opened the door and brought in three bottles of water so cold the plastic was beaded in condensation.

"Thank you," Lilliana said as she took one and opened it.

By this time, Nancy had removed her sweater and laid it in her lap. After a few sips of water, her face had become less flushed.

"Feeling better now?" Cartwright asked her.

Nancy nodded.

"Why don't you tell me exactly what happened on the Fourth of July?"

"But I already told you everything."

"I just want to make sure I've got all of it clear in my mind."

Lilliana thought it more likely the chief wanted the story clear in Nancy's mind. She herself would be interested in the retelling in light of what Rebecca had said.

He put a tape recorder on his desk. "Do you mind if I record your statement? That will make it easier for DeeDee to type it up."

"I suppose that would be all right." She looked at Lilliana for reassurance. Lilliana gave a slight nod of her head.

Nancy repeated the story of going to use the toilet after the fireworks show and then finding Fox Fordyce after she'd been shot. "I'm not sure why I picked up the gun." Nancy's face crumpled.

"Are you sure you didn't see Fox Fordyce earlier?" Lilliana asked.

The chief quickly shifted his eyes to hers. Lilliana avoided his gaze.

Nancy looked confused. "Well, of course I saw her earlier. We were all at the school, listening to the band and eating hot dogs and…"

Lilliana gentled her voice. "I mean right before you got up to use the portable toilet. Are you sure you didn't see her go in that direction first?"

"I don't think so." Nancy closed her eyes, as if trying to

envision the scene that night. When she opened them, she said, "No, I'm sure of it. I left my seat before the last burst of fireworks had finished. Everyone else was still watching them."

"Is there anything else you want to tell me?" Chief Cartwright asked.

Again Nancy looked in Lilliana's direction, as if she would know the answer. Of course, she didn't, so Nancy returned her gaze to the chief. "No."

Chief Cartwright flipped off the tape recorder. "I'm going to have DeeDee type this up right away so you can sign it. You can wait in the lobby until she's done."

Nancy got up, and Lilliana started to rise with her.

"Not you, Mrs. Wentworth. If you wouldn't mind, I'd like to ask you a few questions."

She sank back into her seat while Cartwright brought Nancy and the tape to the lobby. He closed the door on his return.

"Would you like to tell me why you asked Mrs. Gardner if she'd seen Ms. Fordyce go to the toilets?"

If she answered the chief's question directly, the answer was no. But she didn't think he was actually asking her what her preference was. She supposed there was no way around it; she'd have to tell him. "One of the other residents at the retirement home, Rebecca Cushing, told me she was sitting with Nancy during the fireworks show. She specifically said the two of them saw Fox head toward the back of the school yard. She also said Nancy announced her intention to follow her."

"Now why would she do that?"

She had been hoping to leave Christopher out of it, but the chief didn't seem inclined to let her. Lilliana sighed. "We have a new resident at Rainbow Ranch—Christopher MacAlistair. Several of the ladies have designs on him, including both Nancy and Rebecca. They seemed to think Fox was also interested in Mr. MacAlistair."

Chief Cartwright eyed Lilliana. "Seemed to me Mr. MacAlistair 'had designs' on you."

"He offered to walk me back. Mr. MacAlistair is a gentleman and didn't want a woman walking home alone so late at night." She hoped the police chief would buy her story and not ask her any more questions on that topic. Hoping to divert him, she asked one of her own. "Have you gotten results from any of the forensic evidence yet?"

He leaned back in his chair. "The autopsy only confirmed what we already knew. Fox Fordyce died from a gunshot wound to the chest. It will be a week or more before we have results on the fingerprints on the gun or the ballistics report that will confirm the gun was the murder weapon."

"I certainly hope they find some prints that belong to someone other than Nancy," Lilliana said.

"Believe it or not, so do I. Mrs. Gardner seems like a nice lady, even if she is a little ditzy at times." Cartwright tapped his pen on his desk, and Lilliana wondered if she should join Nancy in the lobby. Finally he said, "It's not like the murder is the only problem I have right now."

"Oh?" She tried to encourage him by looking interested and sympathetic.

"It might not sound like as big a crime, but the parents of Rainbow Ranch are sure up in arms about it. Some of the kids have reported seeing a little man hanging around the school.

They say he looks like Robin Hood. Wears some kind of green tunic and has long hair.

"A few of the girls say he plays hide-and-seek with them, ducking behind the playground equipment and disappearing. Sounds like some kind of perverted midget to me." He looked glum.

Lilliana was alarmed. She thought she knew who the "little man" might be, and she didn't like it at all. She'd have to see what she could do about that. "I can see why the parents would be upset. That doesn't sound good to me either."

Cartwright shook his head. "No, it doesn't."

There was a knock on the door. When the chief yelled, "Come in," Nancy poked her head inside and held out a sheet of paper.

"DeeDee said you needed to see me sign this."

"I do," Cartwright said. "Come in."

* * *

Lilliana sat next to Willie and picked up the menu card from on top of the plate.

"How'd it go with Cartwright?" Willie asked.

Since she'd had chicken at lunch, she decided on the broiled salmon with rice pilaf and put the card down. "Better than expected. He doesn't think Nancy is the murderer either."

"That's good to hear. Does he have any other suspects?"

The server stopped at their table and took their orders. Lilliana also asked for hot water for her tea. "Not as far as I could tell. I think we made the right decision as far as doing our own investigation."

"Do *you* have any other suspects?"

The server returned with Willie's soft drink and her miniature pot of hot water. Lilliana busied herself with taking an individually wrapped teabag of Earl Grey out of its foil covering and steeping it in the pot. "Not so far. But I haven't actually interrogated anyone yet." She thought of Rebecca and decided another conversation might be in order.

Sarah and Bob Higgins approached their table, and Willie waved them toward a pair of available chairs. "How have you been, Bob?" he asked in a loud voice.

"Eh?" Bob said.

Willie talked louder, "I said, how have you been?"

"Oh. Fine. Fine." Bob sat next to Willie, and Sarah took the chair beside that one.

"Isn't it terrible about that Fordyce woman?" Sarah said. "A body can't be too careful these days. I'm glad Bob and I stayed home. We watched the fireworks in New York on TV." Sarah tilted her head upward from across the table and Lilliana wondered what she was looking at. She didn't have to wait long.

"Is this seat taken?" Christopher's rich baritone asked from behind her.

Not wanting to cause a scene in front of the others and not sure how to tell him the seat was occupied when it was obviously empty, Lilliana directed a weak smile in his direction. "It doesn't appear to be."

"I don't think we've met," Willie said. "Willie O'Mara." He started to push his hand in Christopher's direction then, as if realizing his arm would wind up under Lilliana's nose, pulled it back.

"Christopher MacAlistair. Glad to meet you. And who is this handsome couple?" he asked, turning his gaze on the Higginses.

"I'm Sarah, and this is Bob." Sarah gestured toward her husband. "You're new here, aren't you?"

"That I am," Christopher said.

"How do you like it?" Sarah said.

"I think it's a verra pleasant place to live." Lilliana could feel his eyes on her as he said, "I'm especially enjoying the company of the pretty women."

Sarah tittered, while Lilliana merely felt awkward. Her hunger vanished at the thought of Christopher sitting next to her throughout the meal.

The server returned with Willie and Lilliana's food and took the orders of the others.

"You go ahead and eat," Sarah said. "Otherwise your food will get cold."

She picked up her fork and broke off a piece of the salmon. Her mouth was dry, but the fish tasted very good.

Sarah kept up the conversation. "You're not from around here, are you, Christopher?"

"No, I'm not. I was born in Scotland."

"I've always wanted to visit Scotland," Sarah said wistfully. She glanced at her husband. "I suppose I'll never go there now."

"I went to the U.K. about twenty years ago," Willie said. "It was part of an exchange training program. Spent a week with the Metropolitan Police in London. We even got a visit to New Scotland Yard. It's an impressive facility."

"I've never been there myself," Christopher said, then paused before adding, "Fortunately."

Sarah tittered again, and even Willie smiled. Lilliana wasn't quite sure what Christopher meant. Which was silly, she told herself. She was attributing all kinds of evil motives and characteristics to Christopher when she had no idea what his situation with Fox Fordyce had been.

There was a pause in the conversation as the server arrived with the other meals. Christopher had ordered the salmon as well. Sarah and Bob had chosen the roast turkey with dressing.

"Are you going to the movie tonight?" Sarah asked Christopher.

"Movie?" He raised his eyebrows.

"Yes." Sarah nodded her head. "Every Wednesday, they show a film in the television room on the big screen and serve popcorn. Tonight they're showing *Brigadoon*."

Lilliana's heart jumped. Apparently her subconscious had remembered that when she was wishing for a musical earlier in the day.

"Humph." Bob broke his silence. "Another silly musical. Why can't they show more war pictures? Or John Wayne movies? Better yet, why don't they show a war picture starring John Wayne?"

Sarah patted his hand. "They do sometimes, dear."

"Will you be going?" Sarah repeated, looking at Christopher.

"That depends."

Lilliana felt his eyes boring into her head. She ducked down, hoping to avoid the laser beam of his stare.

"I don't like going to events alone," Christopher said.

"Especially for the first time."

"Oh, I'm sure Lilliana would be happy to go with you," Sarah said. "Wouldn't you, Lilliana?"

There appeared to be no way to avoid it now. Not without raising a bunch of eyebrows. At least there would be lots of people there. It wouldn't be like last night sitting in the gazebo alone with him. She faced him, trying not to be distracted by those deep blue eyes. "Yes, of course. I was just thinking this morning that I was in the mood for a musical."

"Good. It's settled then. What time shall I pick you up?" Christopher asked.

"I believe the movie starts at seven-thirty," Lilliana said.

"That's right," Sarah chimed in.

"Shall we say seven-fifteen?" Christopher asked.

"That should be plenty of time," she answered. She picked at her rice pilaf, then pushed the plate away.

Willie, whose eyes had been following the conversation avidly, asked, "Mind if I eat that?"

"No. Go right ahead," she said.

CHAPTER THIRTEEN

For the first time in weeks Lilliana poked around in her jewelry box, trying to decide which earrings to wear, whether to add a necklace or a bracelet, and wishing she had time to do her nails. In the end, she put on a pair of pearl earrings and closed the lid on the jewelry box. She'd already changed into a pair of dress slacks and a frilly blouse. No sense overdoing it. Or maybe she had overdone it already. Just as she was going to change into a more casual top, there was a knock at her door. Too late. That must be Christopher.

Lilliana's breath caught when she opened the door and saw him. He, too, had changed. Instead of the golf shirt he'd worn at dinner, he now wore a dress shirt and tie. He'd at least made a concession to the casual style of dress Arizona preferred by not wearing a jacket. But he still looked wonderful. He really was a handsome man.

"Are you going to ask me in?" he asked with a wink. "Or are you going to continue to stand there with your mouth open?"

"I'm ready to go," she said. She wasn't sure she wanted him

inside. Just the two of them alone in her apartment. She felt a shiver run up her spine and stepped into the hall, closing the door firmly behind her.

They were quite early, as the retirement home started the film ten minutes after the announced show time to allow for late arrivals before lowering the lights. Lilliana had forgotten that or she would have told Christopher to pick her up later. At Christopher's suggestion, they sat in the last row after filling a bag with popcorn. Everyone who came to the movie saw she and Christopher were together. She could just imagine the way tongues would be wagging over breakfast tomorrow.

Rebecca came in with Pieter Joncker. That was certainly an odd couple. Although roughly the same age, Rebecca was frail and looked like an old woman, while Pieter had the sturdy body of a Wisconsin farmer, which is what he had been before moving to Arizona. While Pieter's remaining hair was white, including that of his mustache, his eyes were bright and, from what Lilliana had seen of him, he was also energetic.

It also relieved her mind somewhat. If Rebecca and Pieter had started dating, perhaps Rebecca wouldn't be jealous of her sitting with Christopher. And there'd be another couple to occupy those with the wagging tongues.

Nancy came in next, sans Lenny. She and Mary Boyle had probably been held up by Mary's slow progress with her walker. Mary, who led the way, gave Lilliana a big smile. Nancy's face couldn't decide whether to sag or snarl. When her eyes met Lilliana's, she turned away and held her chin high.

Lilliana flinched as her fingers brushed Christopher's while pulling a kernel of popcorn from their shared bag. It wasn't the first time. Each time it happened a spark of electricity jumped between them, stirring feelings she thought she'd left behind in her younger years. He'd asked if she wanted her own bag, but she'd declined, knowing she wouldn't eat all of it herself. Now she wondered if she'd made the wrong decision.

At last the lights dimmed, and she hoped the other women would stop looking at her and Christopher and focus on the film.

Sarah had been mistaken about the movie. It wasn't *Brigadoon*. It was *Finian's Rainbow*. The songs were magical, and Lilliana found herself humming along. Until Christopher caught her at it and smiled at her. She'd flushed and cleared her throat, acting as if that was what she'd meant to do all along.

She wondered if his singing voice was as expert as his piano playing. She'd always considered her own voice rather weak, especially since she'd gotten older. Too often it cracked or faltered. But she did enjoy singing.

The only part of the movie which wasn't wonderful was when Og, the leprechaun, sang "When I'm Not Near the Girl I Love," because it made her think of Sam's story of how Christopher came to town with Fox Fordyce. Had he only stayed in Rainbow Ranch because he hoped to get back together with Fox? And was she herself only the girl that was near, a fill-in while he waited? What would have happened if Fox hadn't been murdered?

Fortunately, the film moved on and so did Lilliana.

A smattering of applause broke out at the end of the movie, when as in all good fantasies, all problems are solved, and the romantic couple gets their happily-ever-after. *If only life were as simple.*

Christopher seemed in no hurry to go, letting most of the others pass them by before rising from his seat. He extended his hand to her and she took it, not because she needed the assistance, but because she wanted to touch him again.

"Would you like a nightcap?" he asked as they walked toward the exit.

She tried to think of where one would get a drink in Rainbow Ranch. The only possibility was the hotel, but she didn't think it had a bar or a restaurant. Cathy's Café didn't serve alcohol and closed after dinner. "I don't think there's anywhere to get one."

"Of course there is. I have several selections in my townhouse. If you don't like any of them, I suppose I could make you a cup of that Earl Grey tea you like so much."

She was surprised he'd noticed what kind of tea she drank. The surprise was probably causing that little squeezing feeling in her chest. Certainly it couldn't mean anything else. "Oh, I wouldn't want to impose on you."

"It would hardly be an imposition." His voice was soft and deep, almost purring, as he looked down on her.

By now they were standing in the lobby, with the remainder of the movie attendees dribbling by on their way to their apartments. The receptionist had gone home for the day. In a few moments, they were the only two remaining. Alone.

They'd be more alone is his casita. The idea both excited and frightened her. "I don't think that's a good idea."

"Why not?" he asked, and the look on his face said it was his turn to be surprised. When she didn't answer right away, he added, "Have I done something wrong, Lilliana?"

She wasn't sure she knew how to respond to that question. The answer depended on what his relationship to Fox Fordyce had been. But that wasn't something she wanted to discuss in the lobby of the Rainbow Ranch Retirement Community, where anyone might walk through at any moment. She wished she could let it go, but she knew she wouldn't rest until she knew the answer. "Maybe we should have that nightcap."

They walked in silence through the warm night, dark skies sprinkled with stars overhead, tiny electric lights along the path below to show the way. The slight breeze carried a hint of monsoon moisture, and Lilliana wondered if they'd have a storm tonight.

The trip between the main building and the row of casitas was all too short. Before she knew it, they were standing on the tiny porch, and Christopher was unlocking his door and holding it open for her.

She stepped inside and took a look around, getting her bearings. Christopher turned left into the tiny kitchen. At the end of a short hall, the casita opened up into a dining and living room area, where the piano was. Where she'd been a few days ago. She followed Christopher.

He opened a cabinet next to the refrigerator, displaying an assortment of bottles. A shelf above held glasses of various types. "Scotch, brandy, bourbon, or sherry?" he asked. "I might also have a bottle of wine or two in the wine rack in the dining room."

Lilliana shrank from the idea of the two of them sharing a whole bottle of wine. It sounded too romantic. And held too many possibilities. "A glass of sherry would be fine. If you wouldn't mind, I'd like to use your powder room."

"I wouldn't mind at all," he said as he reached up and pulled two glasses off the shelf.

Lilliana flushed the toilet, washed her hands, then stood for a moment staring at herself in the mirror. *When had she turned into an old woman? Where had those wrinkles come from?* She didn't mind the white hair. Not too much, anyway. She did mind the tense look around her eyes. She knew she was stalling, avoiding what had to happen tonight. She sighed, then straightened her shoulders and opened the door.

"Everything all right?" Christopher was pouring scotch over the ice cubes that filled an old-fashioned tumbler. A delicate glass of sherry already sat on the counter.

"Fine." She picked up the sherry, fighting to control the trembling in her hand.

Screwing the top back on the bottle of scotch, Christopher picked up his glass. "Shall we sit on the patio? It's such a lovely evening, and I prefer air to air conditioning."

She nodded her assent and led the way to the patio door, which Christopher opened for her. It was nice to meet a man who acted like a gentleman. So many men didn't, leaving you to open your own door and pull out your own chair, with the excuse of being modern. Lilliana tended to think of it as rude and lazy.

She sat in one chair, Christopher in the other, with a small table between them. She was glad for the distance. She took a sip of her sherry and put the glass on the table. Neither of them spoke as lightning danced over the Little Dragoon

Mountains.

The ice in Christopher's glass rattled as he took another drink, then put his glass down. The scotch was almost precisely half gone, as if he'd used it to measure how long he should wait before questioning her again.

"You've seemed a little distant today," he began. "If I've done something wrong, I'd like to know. Women seem to think men can read their minds, but I for one am very bad at that."

She picked up her sherry and took another sip. This time she didn't put the glass down, instead holding it in her hands, stroking the sides with her fingers as if seeking comfort from it. "I took a walk into town today."

A roll of thunder echoed in the distance, not loud, but ominous nevertheless.

"I was told you came to Rainbow Ranch with Fox Fordyce. The person who said that also said you lived with her a while before suddenly moving here."

"That's true."

She waited a beat for Christopher to elaborate. When he didn't, she drank the last of her sherry before continuing. Dutch courage it used to be called. But whatever its nationality, she could use some at the moment. "It made me wonder if you were one of those men who skips from woman to woman, never letting any one of them grow too close, never wanting to commit to a relationship." She put the glass down. He picked his up. "Or whether it was the opposite. Had the two of you spent some time together traveling? Did you leave on your own? Or did she throw you out?"

She took a deep breath. "The thing is, you're the kind of

man who attracts women. You can have your pick. Just ask any of the women living here." She flashed him an ironic smile. "I can't quite imagine why you've decided I'm the one you want to spend time with."

By the time she finished speaking, her head was throbbing with the pounding of her heart.

He finished his scotch. "Do you want another drink?"

"No. No, thank you." Her mouth was dry as ashes.

"Well, I do. I'll be right back." He went inside, leaving her wondering.

Did he need time to make up a story? Or was he just composing his thoughts? A stroke of lightning spider-webbed the sky. The thunder was louder this time.

Christopher returned with a fresh drink and sat down. He'd removed his tie. "I suppose there was no hope of keeping my relationship with Mrs. Fordyce a secret. Small towns spread gossip faster than the Internet."

That was certainly true.

The storm appeared to have cleared the mountains. Stars above them winked out as the clouds covered them.

"It's not what you think. I met her in Aspen. Skiing. She'd come up from Denver for a week. It was the end of the season, and there weren't many guests there. We seemed to run into one another everywhere. After a few days we gave in to the inevitable and met intentionally. Traveling alone enables you to meet many people. But you usually don't become friends.

"Mrs. Fordyce and I became friends. She told me she intended on coming back to Rainbow Ranch. I told her I'd never seen Arizona. She asked if I'd like to go with her."

Lilliana jumped as lightning struck close by, the thunder booming almost simultaneously. Big drops plopped on the surrounding terrain, got smaller and more frequent until the rain came down in torrents, punctuated by bolts of lightning and cracks of thunder.

"Mrs. Fordyce was not well."

Lilliana had almost forgotten Christopher while caught up in the power of the storm. His voice surprised her.

"She'd broken many bones, had many injuries in her rodeo career. She put up a brave face, but she didn't look forward to the long drive. Said her body ached when she sat still for very long. I agreed to come, take over half of the driving."

During their softball practice, Fox had shown no signs of that kind of pain. Had she truly been injured—or exaggerating in order to convince Christopher to travel with her?

As the rain came down in sheets, the thunder and lightning came less frequently. Lilliana shivered. The temperature must have dropped twenty degrees in the last ten minutes.

He must have noticed the shiver. "Do you want to go inside?"

The wind shifted, blowing the rain in on the covered patio, just when she was about to tell him no. Instead she got up. "I think we'd better."

Once inside, she realized there wasn't anywhere to sit except the love seat. She sat at one end, snuggled in the corner, and held out her glass. "I think I'd like a little more sherry now."

He took the glass, a mixture of regret and amusement in his eyes. He wasn't gone very long before returning with her drink.

She noticed he'd refilled his scotch again.

He sat on the other cushion, not too close, yet not too far away.

"When we got to Rainbow Ranch, she offered to let me stay with her. Since the only alternative was the hotel—unless I wanted to become a permanent resident—I accepted her offer. For a while, it worked out well for both of us. I helped her with getting settled. She gave me a place to stay." He paused and stared at his glass, but he wasn't seeing the glass from what Lilliana could tell. "One day she got something in the mail that upset her. She wouldn't tell me what it was, but after that she started complaining that I was 'mooching' off her, and that I either had to start paying rent or move out.

"I decided to move out. Relationships aren't static. They either grow closer or more distant. It was time to move on. And that's the story of me and the redoubtable Fox Fordyce." He took a long swallow of his drink.

She sipped her sherry. His story sounded reasonable. She *wanted* to believe there had been nothing romantic between Christopher and Fox. *Needed* to believe there hadn't been. Which scared her. She decided to accept his version of the events. At least for now. "Would you play the piano for me?"

"I will if you promise you'll sing."

"Oh, I couldn't sing. I'm not very good," Lilliana protested.

"Your voice sounded lovely to me during the movie," Christopher said.

"Well, I suppose…"

He took her hand, pulled her up off the love seat, and led her to the piano bench. Much to her surprise, he started playing "How Are Things in Glocca Morra." She hadn't expected him to know show tunes. She gladly started singing. He joined in with his rich baritone toward the end. Then he segued into "If This Isn't Love," a sprightly tune, and finished up with "Look to the Rainbow," a song somehow appropriate for two people who lived in Rainbow Ranch. As he finished with an arpeggio, he lifted his hands off the keyboard, put them on her shoulders and pulled her toward him. She hesitated just for a second, then leaned into his kiss.

CHAPTER FOURTEEN

The next morning Lilliana got up early, despite the late night. She hummed to herself with a smile on her lips as she got dressed. After the kiss, Christopher had walked her back to her apartment. The rain had stopped by then, and she imagined had the sun been out, there would have been a rainbow. As it was, the Milky Way glowed overhead in the clear, dark sky.

She wanted to go see Esmeralda first thing this morning, before anyone was up. Especially Christopher. She was afraid if he saw her passing his casita, he'd either invite her in or ask to go hiking with her. She'd have to turn him down without explanation, which could possibly put him off. She didn't want to ruin the way things had been between them last night.

She'd wait for tea until she got back. She'd miss her quiet morning cuppa, but it was imperative she leave as early as possible.

She gasped as she passed her kitchen. What had been a tidy little space the night before was now chaos. Cabinets stood open, with cans and jars and boxes spilled out all over the countertop. Sugar from the upturned sugar bowl covered her stove. The roll of paper towels had been unwound, white sheets trailing across the floor.

She had a feeling she knew the source of the problem. She didn't take time to clean up the mess. She could do that after breakfast. Meanwhile, it was even more imperative that she get to Esmeralda this morning.

Christopher didn't see her, but Frank waved from the rear of the last casita on the other end of the row of townhouses. She thought Frank would have given up smoking by now, but she could see the thin plume of smoke rising from the hand that held his morning cigarette. She waved back, wondering how early she'd have to start her hike to avoid him.

The air was still cool after last night's rain, and she made good time getting to the cave. Unfortunately, the entrance was particularly muddy for the same reason, but it couldn't be helped.

"Lilliana," Esmeralda exclaimed when she arrived in the cave room where the fairies lived. "I didn't expect to see you so soon again."

"Is it a bad time?" Lilliana asked. "I could come back tomorrow."

"It wouldn't be any better tomorrow," Esmeralda said sadly.

"What's wrong?"

"I'm afraid Tam Lin is bored," Esmeralda confided. "He doesn't like being shut up in the cave all day. He's used to the forests and fens of Scotland. He's started playing tricks on the other fairies."

She'd been right about the source of the problems. "He's

also started playing tricks on humans."

"What do you mean?" Esmeralda asked.

She told her about the tricks Tam Lin had played, mentioning Willie's wafers and the more serious situation with the children on the playground. At the end, she described the state of her kitchen. She tried to minimize the disarray, but that didn't stop Esmeralda from being distraught.

"I'm so sorry, Lilliana. I've already scolded him, but it doesn't seem to have done any good. I'll talk to him again. I promise I'll send the brownies every night to clean up your kitchen if he's messed it again."

"That won't be necessary," Lilliana said. "It's not just the mischief. I'm afraid someone will catch on to the fact that it wasn't done by humans. It wouldn't do to have people come searching for you."

"You must let me know if it happens again," Esmeralda said.

Lilliana paused. "I'm not sure how often I can come to you now. People have started to notice how I take early morning hikes. I'm not sure if they've noticed my muddy clothes on return, but it would make those who did suspicious."

"Then we'll have to come to you," Esmeralda said. "I'll send Uaine in the morning to check on things."

"She'll have to be careful not to be seen."

"She will. Her green blends in with nature, so people are less apt to notice her."

"I'd better get back," Lilliana said. People other than Frank were likely to be stirring about by now. "I'll tell Uaine if anything more untoward happens."

"I do apologize, Lilliana. Please be careful."

"I will."

* * *

Cathy gave Lilliana and Jaclyn a big smile when they walked in the door before hurrying over to escort them to a booth.

"Haven't seen you in a while," she said to Lilliana.

A pang of grief pricked her heart. She hadn't been back to Cathy's Café since Ted died. Subconsciously there must have been too many memories of meals shared with him here. It was only fitting that she reacquaint herself with the restaurant in the company of his great-granddaughter. She forced a smile to her lips. "The absence will only make your good food taste better."

They slid into opposite sides of a booth near the window. Lilliana picked up the menu. It was unchanged, save for a sheet of paper labeled "Specials" clipped to the inside. The featured offering was liver and onions. That wasn't something served in the dining room at the retirement home very often. In fact, she doubted it would ever be served there, even though she was sure many of the residents, being of a generation used to eating meals other than chicken and hamburgers, would appreciate it. But liver tended to be an acquired taste. One which Lilliana had acquired long ago, and she decided that's what she'd order.

Jaclyn, like her great-grandfather before her, had apparently memorized the menu from eating so many meals here. She didn't even bother to pick it up, much less open it.

Cathy saw Lilliana put her menu down and hurried over, order pad in hand. "What can I get you?" She wrote down Lilliana's order, then queried Jaclyn. "The special?"

Jaclyn nodded.

"How does she know which special?" Lilliana had noticed five choices on the Specials menu.

Jaclyn laughed. "It's my special. I almost always get a burger and fries for lunch."

The café was crowded for a weekday lunch. Most of the residents of Rainbow Ranch commuted to Bisbee or Benson or even Tucson during the work week, so fewer people ate there at midday than at breakfast and dinner. The hum of conversation filled the air as diners chatted over their meals—until one female voice yapped like an angry Pomeranian.

"Is that why you asked me to lunch? To pump me for information about poor Mrs. Gardner?"

Lilliana recognized the voice and searched the tables for its owner until she spotted the clinic nurse from the retirement home sitting with Biff Buckley at a booth in the back. Kirstie, rider of Harley-Davidson motorcycles and wearer of tattoos, wasn't a woman to be trifled with. Her face hardened and her eyes narrowed as she faced off against the television reporter.

Buckley, his back to Lilliana and Jaclyn, spoke too softly for them to hear his response, but she imagined it was conciliatory by the way Kirstie reacted. That was not good news, as far as Lilliana was concerned.

She had a different match in mind for Kirstie, had tried to encourage her to consider Chief Cartwright, but Kirstie had had other ideas. So had the chief. Now she wondered…

Cathy brought their meals, Jaclyn's a plate holding a huge burger on a bun and a mountain of french fries, Lilliana's a slice of sautéed liver with two strips of bacon and fried onions on top, accompanied by mashed potatoes and a serving of peas. She cut a slice off and ate it while Jaclyn took a large bite out of her burger. The girl must have inherited her great-grandfather's metabolism if she ate that every day. Lilliana was pleased that the liver was perfectly cooked and tender. It didn't have any of the nasty tendons in it that liver sometimes did, and didn't taste at all bitter. Of course, Cathy bought quality ingredients, and her chef obviously knew how to cook them. Lilliana settled back to enjoy her meal.

There were no further outbursts from the far corner of the café. Everyone had gone back to their food. But apparently, even though Kirstie and Buckley hadn't disrupted the restaurant again, they still hadn't settled their differences. Kirstie looked disgruntled as she and the reporter passed by on their way out.

"So how are things going with you and our handsome Chief of Police?" Lilliana asked Jaclyn in what she hoped was a casual tone of voice.

Jaclyn blushed. "I'm afraid that didn't quite work out."

Lilliana struggled hard to not blurt out "Good!" Last month, she had tried to play matchmaker. She thought Kirstie and the chief would make a much better pairing than Kirstie and Biff or Jaclyn and the Chief. "Is there anyone else?" she asked instead.

"Not at the moment. I'm really too busy with the store to have a love life right now." Jaclyn sounded wistful. Then, with a mischievous look in her eyes, she asked, "How about you?"

Lilliana felt the hot blush turning her cheeks pink. That tactic had certainly backfired.

Jaclyn's eyes widened. "No. Tell me! No, let me guess." She stared off into space for a moment.

Lilliana put her fork down, her throat too tight to eat.

"I know! That man from the African Violet Club who grew those beautiful plants I saw at the show. Frank? It is Frank, isn't it?"

Lilliana shook her head. "I don't know why you think a woman my age would be involved in a romance."

"What's age got to do with it?" Jaclyn was genuinely surprised. "My great-grandfather and great-grandmother loved one another like Romeo and Juliet until the day she died. Even after that, my great-grandfather couldn't think of getting involved with another woman." Then, realizing who she was talking to, she added, "Until he met you, of course."

"Oh, tosh. We never had a romantic relationship." That was easier to deny since, technically, they hadn't. She and Ted had become friends, had been on the verge of something, but hadn't had time to find out what exactly that something was.

"But you do now," Jaclyn insisted. She picked up another french fry and chewed it thoughtfully. After she swallowed, she said, "It couldn't be that guy who works out all the time."

Lilliana knew she was referring to Lenny, who after retirement, had determined to be the Arnold Schwarzeneggar of the retirement set. She shook her head.

"Sam? I don't think he's a good choice," Jaclyn said of the newspaperman. "He's fairly set in his bachelor ways at this point."

Lilliana picked up her glass of iced tea and examined the ice cubes as she took a slow sip. "No."

She lifted her gaze from her study of the ice. Jaclyn looked as if she were on the verge of bouncing up and down in her seat.

"Don't tell me it's that distinguished Christopher MacAlistair?"

Her blush, which had started to fade with all the wrong guesses, set Lilliana's cheeks on fire. Fortunately, most of the lunchtime crowd had left by now, so there were few people to see it.

"It is, isn't it?" Jaclyn's grin proverbially stretched from one ear to the other.

Lilliana started to shake her head, then stopped and nodded instead. "We've only had one date," she explained. "I'm not sure that qualifies as a relationship yet." But there had also been one kiss. *Did that make it a relationship?*

The grin faded, changed to a studious look. "I'm not sure I should tell you this, but someone has to."

The tightness in Lilliana's throat had eased. Now it was replaced by the clench of her gut. "Tell me what?" *What could Jaclyn know that she didn't? What secrets might Christopher be keeping from her?*

"Mr. MacAlistair was living with Fox Fordyce up until a month ago," Jaclyn said. "I heard she kicked him out. I never heard the reason, but there might be something about him that isn't as nice as his looks."

Lilliana was relieved. "Oh, that. Christopher explained all about that."

Fortunately, when Lilliana didn't disclose any further information, Jaclyn didn't press for it. Lilliana resumed eating her liver, but it had turned cold and wasn't as appealing as it had been just a few minutes ago. The taste reminded her of all the bad things people said about liver. She might have to agree with them in the future.

CHAPTER FIFTEEN

A few days later, Lilliana entered the library carrying her best Royal Purple African violet plant for the monthly club meeting. She was happy to see a good turnout, whether it was because of the ad she'd taken out in the paper or interest in the topic. With any luck the group might soon become large enough to consider becoming a chapter of the African Violet Society of America.

Speaking of which, just as Lilliana set her plant down on the table, Beverly, the receptionist, stuck her head in the door. "Joan MacLeod is here for you."

"I'll be right there."

Joan MacLeod was a petite, perky sixty-year old accredited by the African Violet Society of America as a master judge. "Joan, thanks so much for coming today."

The judge from Tucson wasn't the only one in the lobby when Lilliana went to greet her. Penny Cameron was standing just inside the entrance as well.

"Good morning, Penny," Lilliana said. "Can I help you with

something?"

"I thought I'd come to the African Violet Club meeting today, see what it's about," Penny said.

"Then you're just in time. This is Joan MacLeod." She pointed to Joan, even though the gesture wasn't necessary. "Joan, this is Penny Cameron. Penny has just opened a new flower shop in Rainbow Ranch."

After brief greetings, the three of them headed to the library, which had gained a few more occupants.

"Lily!" Lenny called out.

"Good morning, Leonard," Lilliana said, purposefully using his full name, not that it would be noticed by Lenny. She did wish he would stop calling her Lily.

Sarah had taken her place as president at the head of the table. She'd brought a fancy wooden gavel this time, which she rapped on its sound block. "Order, order."

Those who hadn't already claimed a chair did so now. Lilliana scanned the faces and the plants. Frank had brought his latest cultivar, a pretty yellow one, while Mary had somehow managed to bring three of her miniatures. Pieter Joncker hadn't brought any plants; neither had Rebecca or Nancy. She was surprised to see the two women there, since as far as she knew, neither one of them owned an African violet, much less raised them, although Nancy attended on occasion for the companionship. And to share her baking. Lilliana mentally grimaced. Then she thought of a reason that had nothing to do with plants to explain why they'd decided to come. If Lilliana were a betting woman, she would have given long odds that they were hoping Christopher would show up.

That wasn't going to happen, and she hoped the ladies wouldn't run out the door as soon as they realized that. She had told Christopher about the meeting at dinner last night, just as information, not because she expected him to come. He considered it for a moment, then declined, saying he wasn't good with plants and needed to go into town anyway.

"I call this meeting of the Rainbow Ranch African Violet Club to order," Sarah said firmly.

Lilliana was proud of her. When Sarah had first been elected president of the club, she'd been somewhat timid, deferring to Lilliana constantly for how to run the meeting and announcements and such. Only recently had the elderly woman developed more self-confidence, to the point where Lilliana could settle back in her role as Programs Director.

"I see we have some new attendees today. Welcome. Why don't you introduce yourselves before we get on with the topic of the day."

Rebecca went first, although it was hardly necessary since she lived in the retirement home and most people knew her already. Then Penny Cameron got to her feet.

"Good morning. My name is Penny Cameron, and I own Cameron's Flowers and Gifts. We've just opened a store on Main Street, we being my husband Geoff and myself, and we sell flowers and plants and pots, as well as knickknacks and other little items you might be interested in." She paused and smiled at Lilliana. "I've also taken a few African violets from Mrs. Wentworth on consignment to sell. I sold one yesterday, as a matter of fact."

That cheered Lilliana considerably. She'd been afraid none

of her plants would sell, and she'd ignominiously have to retrieve them from the shop.

"Would you be willing to take plants from other members of the club?" Frank asked.

Penny Cameron eyed the gorgeous specimen sitting in front of Frank. "Certainly," she said. "Why don't you talk to me after the meeting?"

The lift Lilliana had gotten from the thought of a sale sank like a stone. Frank's plants were all prime specimens, and he had so many African violets growing in his plant room. The idea of his plants competing with hers in the shop… well, she had a feeling she'd lose her market unless Penny Cameron sold lots of African violets.

"Lilliana?"

She realized Sarah Higgins had already asked her to introduce the speaker for today once. Just as she was about to do that, Pieter Joncker spoke up.

"Is anyone else going to the pottery class this afternoon?"

"Pottery class?" Nancy said, perking up.

It made sense that Nancy would be interested, since she considered herself artistic. Lilliana thought it might be interesting, although she already had plenty to keep herself busy.

"It's starting today," Pieter explained. "I signed up for it, but not too many others have. If we don't get ten people, they're going to cancel the class. It's free, but you have to pay ten dollars for supplies. They're holding it in the craft room upstairs at two o'clock this afternoon."

At the mention of the ten dollar fee, several interested faces turned disinterested, including Nancy's. Most of the residents didn't have money to spare. A lot of the classes were free, but Lilliana could understand charging for supplies. Ten dollars seemed reasonable for clay and paint and glaze and whatever else one needed to make pottery.

Sarah looked a little annoyed at having been interrupted. Maybe next time she should ask for announcements before starting the program. Lilliana decided to do that before introducing Joan. "Does anyone else have any announcements?"

When no one responded, Lilliana said, "In that case, I'd like to introduce Joan MacLeod. Joan is an accredited judge for the African Violet Society of America. You'll remember she came out to judge our show in the spring, even though we aren't a chapter. After the show, some members asked how the winners were chosen, and, rather than try to explain that ourselves, I asked Joan to come for our meeting today. Please welcome Joan MacLeod."

"Good morning," Joan said cheerily. "I'm happy to be here today. Please hold your questions until I finish each topic. You'll find most of them will be answered by what I am prepared to say, and we can save some time in the long run.

"First of all, the maximum point value for a plant is one hundred. We divide the points into categories and judge each of the categories separately."

She looked around the table. "I'm glad to see that several of you have brought plants to the meeting. Frank, could you pass that lovely yellow specimen up to me?"

Joan waited while the plant made its way to the head of the

table. "The first thing we look at while judging is symmetry." She tilted the pot forward so the members could see the plant head-on. "Ideally, the leaves should form a perfect circle. Leaves of one level should all be of the same size and there shouldn't be any spaces where you can see the soil or table below. The space might indicate a missing leaf."

Seeing the looks of dismay on the faces of her audience, Joan added, "Perfect symmetry is very difficult to achieve. Plants are individuals, and growing conditions can affect symmetry dramatically."

Lilliana could vouch for that. While she grew all her plants under artificial lighting, which did make the plants more symmetrical because the light came evenly from all directions, her leaves tended to be of different sizes, and grooming damaged leaves from them would often leave those gaps Joan spoke about.

As if reading her mind, Joan continued, "The next category is condition. This includes removing any leaves that are faded and tired, snipping off nubs from pinched off leaves or faded blossoms, and keeping the remaining leaves dust free. Oh, yes, faded blossoms are considered a condition problem, so you need to remove those."

Mary looked down at the three small plants in front of her. After a furtive glance around the table, she moved one back behind the other two.

"Symmetry and condition each count for twenty-five points, so you can see how important they are. That's half of the entire score. Frank's plant has lovely symmetry and he's groomed it very well, so it doesn't display any condition issues."

She picked up the plant and passed it down the row. "Lilliana, could I have your plant next?"

Lilliana nervously handed the Royal Purple to Joan. There were a few oohs and ahhs as members caught site of her hybrid.

"Quantity of bloom is also worth twenty-five points. There should be a minimum of twenty-five fresh blossoms on a plant you're having judged. As you can see, this lovely plant has many more blossoms than that. I'd estimate there are seventy-five to one hundred flowers on this single plant. It wouldn't get more points because it has more blossoms, but it certainly does show better than one with the minimum.

"Fifteen points are allocated to size and type of bloom. Each variety of African violet has its own usual size and type of blossom. If the plant being judged doesn't conform to the size and type, points are deducted."

"Excuse me." Nancy was waving her hand in the air. "What do you mean by type?"

"Ah. That's a very good question. An African violet can have single, semi-double, or double layers of petals. As you can see, Lilliana's is a double." She indicated the two layers of petals on one of the flowers. "Frank, could you hold yours up so the group can see the difference?"

Frank obliged.

"Frank's plant has semi-double blossoms. Both his African violet and Lilliana's have star blossoms, meaning they have five leaves per row. The other kind would be a pansy type, which would have two small lobes at the center."

"It sounds very complicated," Nancy said.

"Sounds silly to me," Rebecca said. "I mean, the flowers are either pretty or they're not pretty. All this semi-double pansy stuff seems like a lot of hooey."

"Perhaps," Joan said pleasantly. "But those of us who raise African violets for show consider the differences very important."

Rebecca sniffed. Lilliana assumed neither Nancy nor Rebecca would be attending any more club meetings, even though she could sympathize. There were days she herself wondered why she had chosen a hobby with such extensive rules.

"The last judging category is color," Joan said. "Again, each variety has its own true color, but often specimens produce blooms that don't match it. There are lots of reasons for that, including a problem with light, fertilizer, or temperature. These are all things that can be controlled by the grower."

Joan handed Lilliana's plant back to her. She sighed softly in relief. She'd been so afraid Joan would find a flaw in her plant. If she had, at least she'd kept quiet about it.

"Last, but certainly not least, your African violet must be free of insects and disease. A plant that shows any evidence of infestation won't be allowed to be judged. It's important to employ good practices, including isolating any new plants before exposing your current ones to them. Once you've determined the new plants don't have any diseases or insects, you can safely remove them from quarantine.

"Are there any more questions?" Joan asked.

Pieter raised his hand. "What about pots? Is one kind better than another?"

"For a show, the pot has to be plain, with no markings or designs on it," Joan said. "As far as growing"—she shrugged her shoulders—"everyone has their own preferences. You'll need to experiment with different kinds and see which works best with your growing conditions and watering and fertilizing practices.

"Anyone else?"

When no one spoke up, she said, "Thank you for having me today. I hope my talk has been informative."

There was a light smattering of applause. "Thank you for coming, Joan. Now we'll take a short break before resuming with regular club business. I believe Lenny has supplied some cookies and lemonade for us," Lilliana said.

Most of the members made for the side table and the snack. Frank made for Penny Cameron. The two of them huddled at the side of the room, probably discussing the consignment arrangement. Lilliana bit her lower lip. She hoped Frank wouldn't steal the customers who might otherwise have bought her plants at the Camerons' shop.

CHAPTER SIXTEEN

The last time Lilliana had been in the craft room, it had been repurposed as an interrogation room. Chief Cartwright decided bringing the witnesses up to the second floor would keep them from wandering away. Or perhaps sneaking away. She tried to remember if she'd ever been in any other of the rooms in the common area on this floor before, but she didn't believe she had.

The craft room occupied part of the same location as the dining room on the first floor, a section to the rear of the elevator. Waist-high shelves circled three walls. On one side, cubbies reminiscent of a kindergarten classroom filled the area below the shelves. Locked cabinets occupied the space beneath the shelves on the other two sides. Several folding tables, the same ones that had been used for the African violet show a couple of months ago, were set up in the center of the room, with three folding chairs on each side.

A petite blonde woman was unpacking things from a cardboard box on a table set at right angles to the others.

Beside her, on a platform of bricks, sat a stainless steel contraption with a large blue panel on the front.

Lilliana joined Pieter at one of the tables.

"Good to see you," he said. "I think we'll have enough people to keep the class going, don't you?"

Lilliana perused the room. Nancy sat at the other table with Bernadine Meade and Harlan Taft, one of the retirement home's nastier residents. With his Parkinson's, Lilliana wondered how he'd be able to form clay pots, much less paint them. Sarah entered the room, trailing a reluctant Bob, and joined them.

The clump of Mary's walker drew Lilliana's attention to the door. Mary smiled at her and headed toward the table she shared with Pieter. Immediately afterwards, Willie's bulk filled the entrance. He looked around, spied an empty chair at Lilliana's table, and headed toward it, his walking stick making a softer clump than Mary's walker.

"Hello, Willie," Lilliana said. "I didn't think you'd be interested in making pottery."

"Gotta do something other than read all day," Willie said. "I can't grow pretty flowers like you, so I thought I'd give this a try."

"I'm glad you did," Pieter said. "Nice to see lots of men in this class."

Willie lowered his bulk to the chair. "I wonder what we'll be making?"

"Probably not a tea service," Lilliana said.

Willie chuckled.

The woman at the front of the room put her empty carton

on the floor and ambled toward a door in the corner. She opened it, revealing a closet, and took a pink smock off a hanger from inside. She put the smock on and now, ready to address the class, stood behind the table at the front and gazed around the room with a smile. "If I could have your attention please?"

Conversation stopped as the class turned toward the instructor.

"My name is Grace Dalton. I'm the art teacher at Rainbow Ranch Elementary School and will be leading this beginning pottery class. It's good to see so many here today."

"I've never made pottery before," Nancy interrupted. "Is it very hard?"

"That depends," Grace Dalton said. "You used to play with clay, right?"

Nancy nodded. "A long time ago."

"What we'll be doing today, and for a good part of this class, won't be so different from that. We're going to use the coil and scrape method to create some simple pots. Then we'll decorate them with paints and fire them in the kiln." She pointed at the blue and stainless steel device Lilliana had noticed earlier. "That will be our first project."

"Will there be more than one?" Pieter asked.

"That depends," the teacher said. "If enough people are interested, we'll try a second one. That will be your choice of another simple pot, or if you feel you're up to it, you might try something a little more challenging."

Grace picked up a pot from the collection on the table in front of her and held it up so all could see. The base color was a creamy gray, with a delicate design of flowers and vines painted on over that. "This is a pot I made from clay I collected in the desert and prepared myself. It takes a lot of work to dig up the clay and blend it with water and sand in the proper proportions, so we'll be using commercial clay in this class."

She picked up a photograph from the table and showed it to the seniors, most of whom appeared to be fascinated by the prospect of making their own pots. "You'll have your choice of six different colors of pugged clay."

The colors ranged from pale beige, through tan and brown, ending with a dark brown with a hint of red in it. Lilliana rather liked the red, but painting designs on it that would contrast with the dark color might be difficult.

Grace put the picture down and picked up a couple of books next. "I'm going to pass these out so you can look at different shapes and designs and get ideas for what kind of pot you'd like to make. I'd recommend something simple to start with." She gave each table a book, and the senior citizens huddled over the glossy pictures.

A half hour later, the class was rolling long ropes of clay on the tables before them. Grace had illustrated the technique of coiling the ropes into a circular form, then using a flat tool to scrape both the inside and outside to smooth the surface, fill in the spaces between coils, and force out the air bubbles hiding in the clay.

Lilliana edged her hands to the right side of her pot, where somehow a bulge of clay had developed. As soon as she tamed that section, she realized the left side had a similar deformity.

What she was creating seemed more like a mutant snake than the component to a work of art.

Her glance toward Pieter on her left turned into an envious stare, and she lifted her hands off the clay. Pieter had already formed a coil about three rows high and was expertly scraping the surface into the base of a bowl.

"You've done this before." It was a statement, not a question.

Pieter looked up at her. "Yah, I have. It was something to do to pass the time during the long Wisconsin winters. Besides"—he grinned before continuing—"the kiln kept the back porch warm enough to sit on and watch the snow fall."

His description conjured up a cozy Currier and Ives picture in her mind. Not that she had any intention of ever being in a place where she could regularly watch snow fall again, mind you. She'd grown too used to the heat of Arizona, her blood thinned so that even seventy degrees sometimes felt cold.

"Of course, I didn't need extra heat on the ranch." A wistful look settled in his eyes, and his hands stopped molding the clay, hovered in the air for several seconds before he resumed scraping his pot.

"Ranch?" Lilliana asked.

Pieter kept his eyes on his creation.

She assumed he hadn't heard her question and went back to rolling her clay. When she had a relatively uniform length, she wrapped it into a somewhat lopsided circle. She pushed it with her fingers until it stood a little straighter, then picked up the scraper. As she pushed against the inside wall, the pot bowed out so far that the middle coil protruded between the other layers. She tried to push it back into place, but only succeeded in shifting more of the clay out of round.

She gave a loud sigh. She knew it was loud, because Pieter looked up from his work.

"Watch me," he said. He dipped his fingers in a bowl of water sitting between them and stroked them against the side of his pot. "You have to keep the clay moist. Not too wet, or it will sag. Not too dry or it will crack."

Pieter picked up the scraper and held it against the inside of his project with the fingers of his opposite hand pressing along the outside. "You have to give it equal pressure from both sides to keep the shape. Work slowly so you can feel if things are going wrong."

Lilliana felt dismayed. Making pottery appeared to be more complicated than she'd thought. "I don't think I can do that like you do."

"Sure you can. It yust takes practice. Squeeze your clay back into a ball. It's almost impossible to fix a pot that's out of shape. Easier to start over with a fresh coil."

She did as he said, dismantling all the progress she'd made, and pushing the coil back into a sphere. It resisted her efforts.

"Use the water," Pieter encouraged.

She did as Pieter had, dipping her fingers in the water, then massaging the clay. Pieter was right. The clay was a lot more cooperative now. She looked up at him as she picked up the scraper again. He gave her an encouraging nod. This time, she did a much better job.

"See, you can do it." Pieter was smiling at her. While Lilliana had struggled to get past step two, Pieter's pot was now fully formed.

"I doubt I'll ever be as good as you are." Then an idea came to her. Penny Cameron had said she thought the African violets would sell better if they were in pretty pots. "Do you think you could make more pots than the ones for the class?"

Pieter's bushy white eyebrows arched in a questioning look, the lowered in concentration. "I might. I'd have to get permission to use the kiln outside of class hours. And I'd have to buy my own clay and paints and glazes. That could be expensive."

"But what if someone paid you for the pots?" she asked. She assumed she could pay Pieter a lot less than Penny Cameron would charge her for the pots in the store.

"I would enjoy that," Pieter said. " My only hobby is raising African violets now, and I don't have as many plants as you or Frank do. I have plenty of time to fill. I think I'd like to make pottery again. But what would I do with the pots?"

"Sell them to me." Lilliana explained her idea, and Pieter seemed agreeable to it. She smiled to herself as she finished shaping her own pot. Handcrafted pots would certainly be a selling point. And a unique advantage over Frank's plants in the Cameron's flower shop.

CHAPTER SEVENTEEN

Only a thin strip of sunlight colored the horizon as Lilliana made her way out of her apartment on her way to the cave the next day. Not wanting to take any further chances, she'd been up before dawn—and before Uaine's arrival—to avoid being seen. She'd skipped her morning cup of Earl Grey and hurried into the desert scrub.

"Lilliana!" Esmeralda exclaimed once she'd reached the fairies' domain. "I didn't expect to see you so soon again." Esmeralda flicked a glance at Tam Lin, who was seated cross-legged beside her, strumming softly on some kind of instrument. "No new trouble, I hope?"

She shook her head so Esmeralda would know it wasn't about Tam Lin this time. "Not that I've heard."

Esmeralda visibly relaxed.

"But I have been thinking about our problem. I can't keep coming here before dawn. For one thing, the more I come, the more likely I am to be seen. For another"—she grimaced—"I really do need my tea in the morning."

Esmeralda looked puzzled. "But I thought we agreed on what to do. Uaine is to come to you each morning and see if there is anything you need."

"But she might be seen as well," Lilliana said. "She can't loiter on my patio every day."

"Then what are we to do?" Esmeralda asked.

"I think I have a solution. I'll set up one of those fairy gardens I told you about. If I need to talk to you, I'll raise the flag on the little mailbox the night before. Uaine can fly by early each morning and see if the flag is up. If it is, she can wait for me. If it's down, she can come back here so she won't be seen."

"That might work," Esmeralda said.

"I think it will," Lilliana agreed. "Now, all I have to do is buy the supplies from the Camerons."

"Camerons?" Tam Lin stopped plucking the strings and looked up at her in alarm. "And who might these Camerons be?"

Apparently, Esmeralda had not told him about the newcomers. "Geoffrey and Penelope Cameron recently arrived in Rainbow Ranch and opened up a flower shop," Lilliana said. "I warned Esmeralda that they were selling fairy gardens, and all of you should stay away from them because you might be seen."

"Warn is right!" Tam Lin said. "The Camerons were the reason me and my troop needed to leave Scotland. I'm sure they followed me."

"But why?" Lilliana asked.

"I think they want to trap us, just like you said," Tam Lin

said. "Think of the money they could get for real fairies in their fairy gardens."

"How did they even find you?"

Tam Lin looked shamefaced. "Well, you see, I might have been a wee bit careless. One time, back in Scotland, Penny Cameron saw me dancing about the heather."

"And, knowing you, you teased her in some way," Esmeralda said disapprovingly.

"Well, I might have. Just a little," Tam Lin admitted. "It was a bit of a game, you know. But, after that, she came back with her husband. She kept trying to prove she'd actually seen fairies. They managed to trap old Elphin, but luckily he was able to escape."

"Is that when you stopped helping them make the magical biscuits?"

"How do you know about those?" Tam Lin asked.

She related the story Penny Cameron had told her, then shook her head. "Maybe we shouldn't be in contact until the Camerons are gone."

"But when will that be?" Esmeralda asked. "If they've opened a shop, they're probably intending on staying."

"Maybe the shop won't be successful. Maybe they'll leave town." Lilliana knew she was grasping at straws. "In the meantime, please, all of you, be careful. Don't leave the cave unless you need to."

"But I will send Uaine each morning," Esmeralda said. When Lilliana opened her mouth to protest, Esmeralda shook her head. "No, Lilliana. We are friends. We must be able to communicate."

* * *

Careful as she'd been, apparently it hadn't been careful enough. Christopher spotted her returning from her visit to the fairies and called out from his patio.

Trying to act natural, she smiled and altered course to meet him. She didn't want to seem unfriendly.

"Some day I'm going to have to join you on one of your morning hikes." Christopher paused. "If I can get up early enough."

"That would be lovely," Lilliana said. Now that she wasn't going to be going in the direction of the fairies, it might be nice to have some company. "I don't usually go this early, but I awoke before the sun and decided to take advantage of that."

"Would you like a cup of coffee?" he asked.

"Thank you, no. I want to change before breakfast. I'll have my Earl Grey then." She stressed the name of the tea.

"Oh, that's right, you're a tea drinker. I used to be, but somehow I've acquired a taste for coffee. See you at breakfast, then?"

"Of course." She turned and hurried back to her apartment, hoping he hadn't noticed how dirty she was from her crawl in and out of the cave.

Two hours later, they were strolling down the driveway of the retirement home together, headed into town. When, over breakfast, Lilliana had mentioned she wanted to visit the flower shop, Christopher said he wanted to stop at Pulaski's and see if they'd gotten in the specialty coffee he'd ordered. Despite her reservations, Lilliana liked to think he also wanted to spend more time with her.

When they got to the grocery, Christopher asked, "Would you like to come in with me?"

"You go ahead. I'll be across the street, picking out pieces for my fairy garden."

Christopher entered the grocery while she continued on. Geoff Cameron looked up from the counter as she entered the flower shop.

"Good morning, Mrs. Wentworth," he greeted her gruffly. "What can I help you with today?"

Penny came out from the back of the store. Her eyes were red and teary, but she pushed a smile onto her face at the sight of Lilliana. "Hello, there. Come to check on your inventory?"

Surprised, Lilliana asked, "Have you sold a plant of mine?"

Penny's smile widened. "Two, in fact. I was thinking of calling you this morning, then I realized I don't have your phone number."

"Oh, let me give it to you now." Penny wrote the number down while Lilliana regretted not calling first. She would have loved to have brought more plants to the store since she was coming into town anyway. "I could bring you some more tomorrow morning. Or this afternoon, if you think I should."

"Tomorrow morning would be fine," Penny said. "It will be too hot later today. In fact, I'm surprised you made the trip. It must be ninety degrees already."

"I'm used to it. And I've decided that I do want one of your fairy gardens."

"I'd be happy to help you with that," Geoff interjected. "Come with me."

Penny's smile faded. She shrugged at Lilliana once Geoff

had passed them, then headed toward the back of the store again.

Lilliana followed Geoff. She would have preferred to deal with Penny. She found Geoff repugnant.

"I suppose you'll want to start with a dish," Geoff said. "Unless you have something at home in mind to use?"

"No, I don't have anything suitable. What about that round red one?" She pointed toward a ceramic dish about twenty inches across. The red wasn't bright, more like a brick color. She had just the table to set it on on her patio.

"Excellent choice," Geoff said.

She had a feeling he would have said the same no matter which container she chose. She already had in mind the pieces she wanted to put in the garden from her last visit, including the little mailbox. As she pointed at them, Geoff took one of each from stock and piled them inside the dish.

"So you plan on attracting the little people," Geoff said. He seemed to be eying her a little too intently for a casual question.

"Oh, I don't know that that's possible." Lilliana laughed. "There actually have to be fairies in order for you to attract them."

"Don't you believe in fairies?" The question hung between them for a beat. Lilliana felt awkward, as if Geoff already knew the answer and was merely waiting for her to confirm it.

Penny came through the door to the back again. "Geoff," she said, "There's someone on the phone asking about payment for a shipment. I told him we hadn't gotten the shipment yet, but he insists you signed for it. I think you'd better talk to him."

"Excuse me, Mrs. Wentworth. Let me put this on the counter for you. It's a too heavy to carry around."

"I'll take that," Christopher said. Lilliana hadn't heard him come in. She supposed Penny had been talking when the bell over the shop door rang. Geoff gave her selections to Christopher along with the same intent stare with which he'd recently been favoring Lilliana. Geoff didn't let go of the dish immediately. It was almost as if the two men were having a tug of war. Or wills.

"Geoff?" Penny said.

He let go and hurried back to where Lilliana supposed the store's office was.

"Are you finished, Lilliana?" Penny asked.

She shook her head. "I suppose I'll need some plants if it's to be a garden. I don't think my African violets will do very well on the patio. Can you recommend some?"

"Of course," Penny said. "Come over this way." Her feet tapped across the cement floor toward a display of small, green plants. "These are all dwarf varieties. They don't grow very fast, so you won't need to prune them very often. You might want to try an English boxwood as a tree." Penny gestured toward a small variegated leaf plant.

Lilliana thought the fairies might like that; it might remind them of home more than the mesquite and palo verde of Arizona. "I'll take one. No, give me two."

"Some dwarf mondo grass or moss would make a nice ground cover." Penny pointed to pots containing those. "Or ajuga." She pointed to a plant with fleshy green leaves, interspersed with a few purple ones.

"That's pretty," Lilliana said. "I think I'll take one of those and some moss."

Christopher, apparently bored with the discussion of foliage, wandered over to the gift area. This gave Lilliana a chance to speak to Penny privately. She lowered her voice to a whisper. "Is something wrong, Penny?"

Penny started to shake her head, then, with a quick glance in Christopher's direction, nodded. "It's Geoff. He's been disappearing for long periods of time lately. And, well, he hasn't been as attentive as he used to be, if you know what I mean."

She almost asked for clarification, then realized what Penny was referring to. "And?"

Penny's whisper became barely audible. "I think he might be having an affair."

"Surely not." Lilliana responded almost as a reflex, then realized Penny had confided in her, genuinely thought there was a problem, and it was uncharitable not to believe her. "Any idea who with?"

"For a while I thought it was Fox Fordyce. I even followed him one night when he went out. He went into the hotel. A few minutes later, Ms. Fordyce arrived. A while after that, they came out together." Penny blinked back tears. "But it can't be her now."

"He's still disappearing?"

Penny nodded. "Sometimes. I'm not sure where he goes. I've been too afraid to follow him again."

She could certainly understand why Penny Cameron thought

her husband had been having an affair. Perhaps he had. But in light of what Tam Lin had said, he might also be hunting for fairies. Since Fox Fordyce had lived in Rainbow Ranch for most of her life, perhaps Geoff thought she might know something about them.

Before the discussion could go any further, Christopher returned. "Are you almost done?" he asked.

She realized the fairy garden components must be heavy. "Almost," she said, then quickly asked Penny, "What about something with flowers?"

Penny looked thoughtful for a minute, then said, "You could add some creeping phlox. This one is a candy stripe—white with pink along the edges of the blooms. But you already have a lot of plants for such a small container. Remember you're going to need room for the house and the bench and the other things."

"Oh, that's right, isn't it?" Lilliana had been so intrigued by the furniture and the plants, she'd forgotten there were limitations. In the end, she put back the ajuga and one of the miniature boxwoods. "That should be all right, shouldn't it?"

"I think it will be perfect," Penny said. "Let me check you out."

Christopher put his burden on the counter, and Penny added the plants she'd picked out. After Lilliana paid her, Penny asked, "Are you sure you don't want me to hold these for you until you can come back with a car or something?"

She thought of the wagon back at her apartment and wished she'd had the foresight to bring it with her. She gave Christopher a questioning look.

"I think I can handle it," he said.

Penny wrapped up the dish in newsprint, put it in one shopping bag, then put all the fairy garden pieces in their boxes in another. She also carefully wrapped the plants and lay them in a third shopping bag, putting strips of cardboard between them and stuffing more newsprint around the edges so the plants wouldn't tip over. "There, that should work."

"I'm sure it will," Lilliana said. She picked up the bag with the plants while Christopher grabbed the other two.

"Ready?" Christopher asked.

"I think so," Lilliana responded.

The July heat was like a slap in the face when they exited the shop. "Maybe I'm not as ready as I thought I was," Lilliana said.

"I'm sure you can make it," Christopher said. "Then we can have a nice leisurely lunch from what I bought at the gourmet grocery."

She hadn't noticed the fourth shopping bag, the one with Pulaski's Gourmet Grocery printed on the side. She couldn't imagine what was in it, but since it came from Jaclyn's store, it was sure to be delicious. And then she realized that Christopher didn't mean to eat in the dining room.

Her heart thudded in her ears. *What would she do if he tried to kiss her again?*

While he'd offered a reasonable explanation for his relationship with Fox Fordyce, the fact that two people thought they needed to tell her about it gave her pause. "Thank you for the invitation, but I think I'd better set up my fairy garden. Perhaps another time."

CHAPTER EIGHTEEN

The next morning, Christopher extended his hand to Lilliana to assist her down the step from the retirement community van. So many residents had been interested in attending the wake for Fox Fordyce, they'd scheduled the van to drop them off and take them back once it was over.

Apparently the retirees weren't the only ones interested in the funeral. A line had formed on the steps on the funeral home. Sam Horn was snapping pictures of the crowd.

Nancy and Mary had hurried ahead with the likely intention of grabbing the best seats possible. Surprisingly, Pieter and Harlan had also come on the expedition, as had Sarah and Bob Higgins, who attended most funerals and memorials. At least she and Christopher had met Fox in life. The others, she was sure, were merely curiosity-seekers.

When she and Christopher reached the entrance, Sam spotted them and waved. While Lilliana smiled back, Christopher turned away. *Did he not want his picture taken? Or did he not want to speak to Sam Horn?*

Once inside, they joined the line snaking its way toward a couple seated near the casket. A man somewhere in his forties, with the same angular build as Fox, sat beside a carefully groomed woman of about the same age. The man looked uncomfortable in a new suit and stiff white shirt. He ran a finger inside his collar every minute or so.

Lilliana tapped Nancy, who was standing ahead of her in line, on the shoulder and asked, "Who is the young man?"

As she'd expected, Nancy, an inveterate reader of obituaries, had already determined the answer to that question. "Tom Fordyce, Fox's son. She only had the one boy. I read he lives in Ohio now. Something about the wife not wanting to move to the desert."

They shuffled forward a few more steps.

Lilliana asked Christopher, "Did you ever meet Fox's son?"

Christopher shook his head, left his eyes averted when he answered. "I didn't even know she had one. I told you we weren't that close." His breathing seemed labored.

"Odd. You'd think a woman would talk about her child." Then Lilliana realized she hadn't said much about Anne to Christopher. But Anne was different, she thought. Anne wasn't alive. And she had only gotten to know the handsome Scotsman over the past week. Surely the subject would come up sometime soon. But if what he'd told her was true, he'd spent several months in Fox Fordyce's company. Surely they would have discussed children in all that time.

"A penny for your thoughts," Christopher's voice whispered in her ear.

"Oh, nothing important." She peered around Nancy's

shoulder to see how much longer they'd have to wait. They'd moved up to the point where there were only three or four people ahead of them. At last they reached the bereaved relatives.

"I'm sorry for your loss," Lilliana said in a rote recitation of what you always said to mourners whom you didn't know very well. "I'd just gotten to know your mother. I'd hoped we could become friends, but unfortunately now that will never happen."

The young man thanked her, and Christopher added his condolences. They moved on.

"Are these seats all right with you?" Christopher waved toward a pair of chairs in an otherwise full row toward the back of the room. She noticed Nancy and Mary seated a couple of rows ahead.

"Fine," she said, and took a seat. Christopher sat next to her. They had been two of the last in line, and Lilliana was glad they wouldn't have to wait long before the service started.

A silver-haired gentleman in a black suit entered the room and stood at the end of the line. When it was his turn, instead of adding his condolences, he leaned down and whispered something in Tom Fordyce's ear. Tom got up and followed him out of the room.

Nancy turned around and said, "I wonder what that was about."

"Probably some minor problem with the service or something," Lilliana said. Nancy stared toward the exit, then asked the same question of Mary, who seemed more than willing to offer opinions, and started telling a story about when her husband died. As long as the funeral service wasn't going to start right away, Lilliana thought she had time for one other thing. She turned to Christopher. "I'm going to find the ladies room. I'll be right back."

He indicated he'd heard her, and she slipped out of her seat and went into the vestibule. She didn't take much time in the restroom, and hurried out the door, hoping the service hadn't started.

And literally ran into Tom Fordyce, who had just come out of a door labeled Funeral Director across the hall. "Oh, I'm terribly sorry," she said.

"It's perfectly all right," Tom Fordyce answered.

"I hope there isn't any problem with the service?"

He shook his head. "No, no problem." He grimaced. "Just more paperwork. I didn't write down the number of copies of the death certificate I needed."

"I'm glad it's nothing serious," Lilliana said, then realizing how what she'd said might be taken, she added, "Not that death certificates aren't serious."

"I'd better get inside so the service can begin." He didn't wait for a response, but rushed off in the direction of the viewing room. Lilliana followed him.

The service was brief. A clergyman in a brown suit read traditional Bible passages and said a few words that sounded as if they could have applied to anyone, interspersed with some canned organ music. The music didn't sound like any hymns Lilliana recognized, more like the background music that used to be played on soap operas. That was probably appropriate. Fox Fordyce hadn't struck Lilliana as the church-going type.

At the end, Christopher leaned over and told her he'd meet her at the van. She assumed he had to make the same kind of trip she'd made before the service. Since she expected to have to wait for him, she didn't hurry to leave the room. They'd made some announcement about meeting at a restaurant afterwards—food following a funeral being one of those mandatory traditions—but most of the retirement home folks didn't have money for restaurant meals.

She passed through the lobby and opened the front door, but the van wasn't parked outside yet. Rather than wait in the hot sun, Lilliana backed up a step or two and stood with the Higginses, making all the usual comments about how good the corpse looked and how nice the service was. She kept glancing up to see if Christopher was coming. The restroom visit seemed to be taking quite a long time for a man. She glanced up once again and was surprised to see him coming not out of the men's room, but out of the funeral director's office. *Whatever had he been doing in there?*

The sound of an engine signaled the arrival of the van, followed by Raul poking his head inside the door to summon the seniors. Lilliana decided to go outside after all. Christopher caught up with her just as she lifted her foot to climb into the vehicle.

"Is everything okay?" she asked him.

"Why wouldn't it be?" Christopher looked surprised.

"No reason." She reached the first empty seat and slid into it so she could sit next to the window. As soon as Christopher was seated beside her, she added, "I saw you come out of the funeral director's office."

"There was a light out in the men's room," he explained. "I thought it might be a safety hazard, and I didn't know who else to report it to."

There wasn't much conversation on the trip back. If Lilliana's own feelings were any indication of the others', going to yet another funeral had reminded them of their own demise, an event that was closer than any of them would like to admit.

It was still too early for lunch when they got back from the funeral. Christopher went back to his casita to change into something more casual, while Lilliana went to her apartment did the same.

For a change, she didn't feel like sitting and reading or grooming her African violets. She felt restless. It crossed her mind to take a stroll to Christopher's casita while she waited for the dining room to open, but she didn't want to seem too eager to pursue their relationship. She wished she could make up her mind. One minute she wanted to spend all her free time with him, and the next she wanted to avoid him.

She decided to wander indoors and see who else might be about. She found Rebecca sitting in one of the easy chairs in the lobby, a crochet hook in hand with a length of white cotton trailing from it to a ball nestled in beside her. It looked like she was crocheting a doily. *Who in the world used doilies any more?*

She sat in the matching armchair close by. "Hello, Rebecca."

Rebecca's lips moved silently as she quickly completed a couple of stitches. "There." She peered over her half-glasses and smiled. "Can't lose count, you know, or the pattern won't come out right."

"Do you crochet a lot?" Lilliana asked.

"Depends on what you mean by a lot. I pretty much always have a project going, but I can't work as long as I used to. My eyes get tired." She took off her glasses and held them in her lap. "Do you crochet?"

"Me? No. I never learned."

"I could teach you," Rebecca said.

"My African violets keep me busy," Lilliana said. *Spending her days crocheting sounded just a little too old ladyish for her.*

"So where was everyone this morning?" Rebecca put her glasses back on and resumed working on her doily.

"Fox Fordyce's funeral. There was quite a large turnout. I wasn't aware so many people knew her. I suppose you're one of the few who didn't."

"Me?" Rebecca snorted. "I knew her all right." The crochet hook flew faster in her fingers.

"Oh?"

"I know I don't look it now," Rebecca said, "but I used to be a rodeo queen myself back in the day."

"So you knew Fox from the rodeo," Lilliana encouraged her.

Rebecca nodded. "That's right. 'Course, I was a little older than she was. I won all the barrel races before she started riding. Did calf roping and bronc riding, too. Back then women competed in all the events, just like the men."

"I didn't know that."

"'Struth. Then Gene Autry came along and said women didn't belong in the tough events. Said they should stick with barrel racing. Well, that's all those men needed to ban us from competing."

"So how old were you when you met Fox Fordyce?" Lilliana was trying to envision the difference in ages. Rebecca looked so old and, yes, feeble, compared to the robust Fox Fordyce. Well, robust a week ago. Not so much now.

"Twenty-five." Rebecca closed her eyes and leaned back, a smile on her lips. "I was beautiful back then. Had all the cowboys after me. Drove the crowd wild, too, with my skirt flying up as I rode around those barrels, encouraging my horse with the crop, hair streaming in the breeze. I was always voted rodeo queen."

Rebecca's eyes opened as her brow formed a frown. "Then Fox came along, sixteen if you believed her. I think she was closer to fourteen. Didn't stop her from competing. If you could call it that."

"What do you mean?" Lilliana asked.

"Well, when she first came up, she used to clock watch to make sure she won her division."

"I'm sorry, I'm not familiar with that term."

"See, barrel racing has divisions by time. So, if you know you're not going to be the absolute fastest, you watch the times of the other horses and figure out how fast you need to go to be first in the slower divisions. You clock watch. Then you hold your horse back just enough to be in a slower division."

"That doesn't sound fair," Lilliana said.

"It isn't. But the rule against it isn't always enforced, even if they catch you at it. Fox, who was always flirting with the judges, rarely got called on it. But that wasn't the worst of it." Rebecca lowered her voice to a conspiratorial whisper.

"What else?"

"Drugs."

"That's got to be illegal," Lilliana said.

"Well, it isn't. Technically. Or wasn't back when Fox and I were racing. She'd take a high-spirited horse, too high strung to compete normally, and shoot him up with tranquilizers so's he could race without knocking over all the barrels. I would never abuse a horse like that. So Fox started winning more than me. After a while, I figured out what she was doing and knew I'd never win again."

"That must have made you angry. Or sad."

"It did," Rebecca said vehemently. "I decided it was time to give up the rodeo. Got a clerical job over to Fort Huachuca. Worked there thirty years. Got a good retirement, too." She smiled.

She might have continued the conversation, but just then Christopher showed up. "There you are. I've been looking for you."

CHAPTER NINETEEN

Lilliana could feel the eyes boring into her as she and Christopher entered the dining room, although every time she turned toward the heat of the laser stares, the person looked away. This was usually followed by a whispered conversation with someone in a neighboring chair. She supposed she should ignore it. Eventually, the retirees would tire of gossiping about the latest couple and move on to someone else. Still, it made her uncomfortable.

Christopher seemed oblivious to the scrutiny. In fact, he made the situation worse by heading for a table for two near the window rather than joining one of the larger tables with other people they knew.

"I thought it might be nice to have a view while we ate," he said as he held out a chair for her.

She smiled as she sat down. The view wasn't spectacular, consisting mostly of the empty tennis courts and the start of the labyrinthine paths that wound their way behind the casitas. She supposed she'd be seeing more of those now that heading off toward the foothills was out of the question. As she remembered, there were periodic rest stops with benches at various points along the way for quiet contemplation.

Once the server had delivered their lunches—a chef's salad for Lilliana and roast chicken for Christopher—he started a conversation. "Do you have any plans for this afternoon?"

Lilliana's heart did a little tha-thump. "I thought I'd start some new plants. Since I've actually sold some in the Camerons' shop, I'd better make sure I have a good supply."

"Oh." He looked disappointed.

"Did you have something else in mind?" She wished her heart wasn't beating so fast.

"As a matter of fact, yes." He cut off a piece of chicken and swirled it in the gravy before lifting his fork in the air. Before putting the food in his mouth, he said, "I saw a flyer near the reception desk about a talent show."

Lilliana had seen that flyer. A copy had been put in every resident's mailbox. Having no talent—other than for growing African violets—she'd tossed it in the trash. But Christopher had talent. "I think you should enter. You play the piano so beautifully."

He chewed his chicken slowly. At last he swallowed. "I was considering it. I was also considering entering as a duet."

What did he mean? Then she realized exactly what he meant. "Oh, I couldn't. My voice isn't that strong. And I'd be frightened of singing in front of people."

"That's why they make microphones. You don't need to sing loud." He drank some iced tea. His eyes met hers over the edge of the glass. "There's nothing to be frightened of. I'll be right there with you."

She found it hard to breathe. Had something gone wrong with the air conditioning?

He put the glass back on the table and cut off another piece of chicken. "Anyway, I thought we might practice together this afternoon, find a song or two we both like." Seeing her reluctance, he added, "You don't have to commit to the contest now. I just thought it might be nice to sing with you again. We can see how it goes." Another pause. "You can decide on the contest later."

An afternoon with Christopher sounded very nice. But she really should work on her plants. If she let them go for too many days in a row, it would be difficult to get back on schedule. Then she chided herself. She knew she was making excuses. Because she was afraid.

She was a self-sufficient woman. She'd had to be since Charles had had his stroke. She'd gotten used to being alone. A twinge grabbed her chest. Not entirely used to it, she had to admit.

"Lilliana?" He was waiting for her answer.

"I'd be willing to try it," she said reluctantly. Then, as joy lifted inside her like a colorful balloon, she smiled and added, "I'd love to sing with you again."

"That's settled then." He smiled in return.

He really did have a magnificent smile. Her smile widened in response, and it wasn't long before the two of them were grinning at one another like two lovesick adolescents.

She didn't even mind when, after they finished eating, he took her hand as they left the dining room in plain sight of the all the residents of the retirement community.

"When is this talent show?" Lilliana asked, thinking about how long they'd have to practice.

"A week from Saturday."

Her body tensed as if a quartet of mischievous brownies had grabbed each of her hands and feet and was pulling on them as hard as they could. "Surely not so soon. We won't have enough time. We have to find the right song, and the right key, and memorize the words, and..."

Christopher burst out in a belly laugh. "You worry too much, Lilliana. We're not performing at Carnegie Hall."

She supposed he was right. She tried a weak smile in response.

They'd reached his casita by this time. He unlocked the door and held it while she entered. Such a little thing, but like pulling out her chair for her, it meant a lot to someone who was raised when manners and courtesies counted for something.

He strode directly to the piano and raised the lid over the keys. She sat beside him, tentative, remembering the last time she'd sat here and they'd sung together. *And kissed.* Better not to think about that part.

He didn't say a word, but launched into a bouncy version of "If I Knew You Were Coming I'd've Baked a Cake," belting it out in dance hall style with a twinkle in his eye. When he finished, he said, "And I would have, too, except as I remember it, you're not one for sweets, are you?"

"Not usually. Except for my gourmet chocolates."

"Ah, that's right," he said. "I'd forgotten about those." He wasn't telling the truth. She knew because he reached into his breast pocket and pulled out a small foil-wrapped square and gave it to her.

It was hard for Lilliana to keep from gasping with delight. Warmth spread through her body. Another little thing. It seemed to her the important things in life were not the big things, but the little things. Too many men tried to impress you with the big things. Television seemed to think a new luxury car was an appropriate Christmas gift. She preferred this one small square of chocolate. It showed he'd taken the trouble to know what she liked. He'd thought about *her* when he picked it out, not the gift itself.

She unwrapped the chocolate square and popped it in her mouth. She closed her eyes as she savored the earthy, rich taste melting on her tongue, sliding down her throat, nestling in her stomach. Slowly she opened her eyes to find Christopher staring at her bemusedly.

"I think I'm going to have to buy you more chocolate." His voice was husky. "Do you mind if I have a taste?"

She didn't trust her voice to answer him, so she moved her head slightly to one side, then the other. He leaned toward her, touched his lips to hers, his arms encircling her. Her arms responded by sliding around his body, pulling him closer. His tongue feathered her lips. Startled, she resisted for a moment. Just as she was about to respond, he gently pulled back, withdrew his sensuous tongue, closed his lips.

"Sweet," he said from under hooded eyes.

If Lilliana thought she'd had trouble breathing before, now she felt as if all of the air had been sucked from her lungs, leaving her empty and filled all at once. She drew in a breath slowly, inhaled it deep inside her, filling the space he'd left behind. "Chris."

It was all she could manage.

"Lil." Unlike Lenny or Fox, whose nicknames had annoyed her, she didn't mind him not using her full name at all. He pushed back a strand of her hair that had fallen over one eye, stroking her face with his gentle fingers, delicate touches that sent chills up her spine.

And then he dropped his hands from her, put them back on the piano keys, and asked in a normal voice, "What do you think we should sing together?"

She'd expected something romantic when he started to play, but instead he launched into "Music, Music, Music," another bouncy song, sung by Teresa Brewer back when they were both young.

"More show tunes?" he asked. "I think I have the sheet music to *The King and I*." He segued into "Getting to Know You." "Or possibly *The Music Man*." His voice boomed out "Gary, Indiana" as his fingers played the melody. She joined in, humming and going "da-da-da" when she didn't remember the words.

The music brought back lots of old memories. In fact, it brought back songs she'd forgotten she knew. "Do you know any Patty Page songs?"

"Like this one?" he asked, as he changed to "How Much Is That Doggy In the Window?" He seemed determined to keep it light after the gentle passion that had been exchanged between them just moments ago.

"That wasn't the one I was thinking of," Lilliana said.

"Surely not this one." He changed to the mournful "Tennessee Waltz."

Tears came to her eyes as he played, memories of times long past flickering on the silent screen inside her head. Chris stopped suddenly, brushed the tears from her lashes. "That's much too sad for us, Lil."

She blinked back the tears. "I should go back to my apartment and tend to my African violets."

"But we haven't chosen a song yet," he protested.

"Another time." She rose from the piano bench and headed for the door. Behind her she could hear the strains of "If I Loved You."

* * *

As Lilliana transferred one shelf's African violets at a time to her workstation, she redirected her thoughts to the unsolved murder of Fox Fordyce. Distracted by Christopher's attentions, she'd been remiss in doing her part to solve the crime. Now she hoped the crime would distract her from Christopher.

Her conversation with Rebecca earlier in the day had added another suspect to her list. From her angry tone of voice and scowling face, Rebecca still held a grudge against the murdered rodeo queen. She'd have to bring that piece of information to Chief Cartwright's attention.

There was also the alleged affair between Geoff Cameron and Fox Fordyce. Usually, where there was smoke, there was bound to be fire. Was Geoff a possible suspect? Was Penny?

Poor Nancy couldn't be ruled out. Not only had Lilliana found her standing over the body with the murder weapon, she clearly had a crush on Christopher. Jealousy was a powerful motive, and if Nancy considered Fox a rival, might she have killed her? If so, Lilliana had better watch out for her own safety.

Which, unfortunately, brought her back to uncertainty about Christopher. Both Sam and Jaclyn had told her he and Fox had had a falling out. Had that "falling out" been much more serious than he'd implied? That might have given him motive. And he certainly had an opportunity when he'd left Lilliana's side.

His story about the burned out light bulb seemed slightly fishy. Did she believe he'd really gone to the funeral director over that?

She wanted to believe him about everything, but, in truth, what did she really know about Christopher MacAlistair?

CHAPTER TWENTY

Another morning, another trip to town. At least she was keeping up with her exercise, despite it being full summer.

After a night's sleep, Lilliana wondered whether yesterday with Christopher had been real or not. It seemed more like a dream, a scene from a movie. She knew it would be all too easy to forget her common sense and be swept away by the handsome Scotsman. She might already have been swept away, but there was still a chance of battling the tide and swimming back to shore.

What was it President Reagan had said? Trust but verify? This morning Lilliana was on her way to verify Christopher's story about his talk with the funeral director.

Fortunately, Mr. Valdez was able to see her immediately. "How may I help you, Mrs. Wentworth?" he asked once they were seated in his office.

The office was very formal, dark shades drawn over the windows, a mahogany desk and bookcases which were empty except for a couple of large loose-leaf notebooks lying on their sides on the lowest shelf.

"I was here for Fox Fordyce's funeral," she said.

"Yes, I remember seeing you." He sounded disappointed.

Had he expected her to make funeral arrangements for herself? Perish the thought. She wasn't ready to die yet. "You do?"

There were so many people at Fox's service, she was surprised he'd taken note of her, especially since she hadn't done anything remarkable that day. Indeed, most days she did nothing remarkable.

"You think I shouldn't remember you? You are a very striking woman."

Mr. Valdez was certainly a charmer. But she didn't want charm today. She wanted information. Fortunately, Valdez moved on, easing the transition to what she came to discuss with him.

"Besides, you were with that man who came to see me later. Mr. ..." apparently Valdez's memory for Christopher wasn't as sharp as for herself.

"MacAlistair," Lilliana supplied. "As a matter of fact, Mr. MacAlistair is why I came to see you."

A look of concern—whether it was genuine or not, Lilliana found it hard to tell—dropped down over Valdez's features like a curtain. "He's not ill, I hope."

"Ill?" She wasn't sure why Valdez would make that assumption. Then she got it. "Oh. Oh, no. Mr. MacAlistair is in robust health." In other words, he wasn't going to die any time soon. At least, she hoped he wasn't.

His face eased, but remained guarded. He picked up a pencil from his desk and turned it round in his fingers. "I'm glad to hear that."

"I believe he came to see you that day." She waited, hoping Valdez would help her out again. He didn't. He merely sat there, fiddling with the pencil, some kind of nervous habit she supposed. "He told me it was something about a light bulb?"

"Light bulb?" Valdez stopped twirling the pencil, held one end in each of his hands so tightly his knuckles whitened. "No. He requested a copy of the death certificate."

Her heart stopped beating for a minute and a wave of vertigo washed over her. *Christopher had lied to her.* As her heart resumed beating and the swirling room steadied around her, she was able to ask, "For himself?"

Before he could stop himself, Valdez nodded. The pencil snapped in two with a loud crack as his grip on it tightened.

She moistened her lips. "Why would someone not related to the deceased need a copy of the death certificate?" She hoped he wouldn't correct her on the "not related" part. Could Chris have married the rodeo queen? If he had been married, he was now a widower. Still eligible. But Fox hadn't been dead when Chris had first flirted with her.

"There are many things that require a death certificate. Probate of a will. Closing of a bank account. All of those reasons are confidential." His face closed down hard. "Unless *you* are related to Mr. MacAlistair? Or Ms. Fordyce?"

"Me? No, I'm not related to either of them." Although part of her had been hoping she might be. "Why did Mr. MacAlistair need one?"

Valdez dropped the two pencil halves into a waste basket beside his desk, brushed his palms against one another. "As I said, that information is confidential."

Lilliana wracked her brain, trying to think of a way to ask for more information without raising the funeral director's suspicions further, but couldn't come up with one. She rose from the chair. "Well, thank you for your time, Mr. Valdez."

"Have a nice day."

What an incongruous thing to say, thought Lilliana.

* * *

As long as she was in town, she might as well stop by Town Hall and see the chief for an update on the murder case.

Poor Chad Cartwright looked like he wasn't having a very good day either. He slumped in his chair, a half-empty cardboard coffee cup and a donut on the desk in front of him. As she entered, he picked up the donut and took an unenthusiastic bite.

"Good morning, Chad."

He shifted in his seat, straightened in an attempt to look a little more professional. "Good morning, Mrs. Wentworth. What brings you in today?"

She got straight to the point. "I was wondering if you'd gotten any results from the crime lab yet."

Cartwright picked up a manila folder from his desk, opened it to a form with Department of Public Safety in large letters across the top. "As a matter of fact, I have."

"And?" Lilliana prompted. Since he'd opened the folder, it was obvious he intended to share the contents of it with her, but sometimes it took a bit of prodding to get him to do what he intended.

"The only fingerprints on the gun were Mrs. Gardner's."

"Well, the criminal must have wiped his prints off it, of course. You honestly don't think Nancy Gardner could have killed her?"

"She can't *always* be innocent," the chief said, referring to the last murder where it had also appeared as if Nancy was the killer.

"Where would she get a gun?" Lilliana asked. "I can't imagine Nancy buying a gun, much less shooting one."

"She didn't have to buy it. She probably borrowed it." Cartwright started to slump in his chair again.

"From whom?" Lilliana asked.

"Rebecca Cushing."

"What? Rebecca must be over eighty years old. Hardly the type to own a gun."

"Apparently she is the type," Cartwright said. "I checked the serial number. The gun is registered to Rebecca Cushing of Rainbow Ranch."

She was about to protest again, then held her tongue. *Was it possible?* Rebecca had been at the fireworks show along with the rest of them. She also had a motive, one the chief probably wasn't aware of.

"You might have something, Chief." Lilliana proceeded to tell him about the rivalry between Rebecca and Fordyce in their younger days, how Rebecca felt Fox had cheated her out of the rodeo queen's crown. "I'd say that was motive."

"But why wait until now?" Cartwright asked.

"Because Fox Fordyce left town. She only came back to Rainbow Ranch a couple of months ago. Rebecca probably learned of her return when the article was published in the paper." Lilliana had almost convinced herself. Apparently she wasn't quite as successful in convincing the chief.

"I'm still having a hard time believing a woman that elderly and not in the best of health could have managed a murder. Now, Mrs. Gardner is no spring chicken herself, but she's in a lot better health than Rebecca Cushing"

She didn't like the way the conversation was going. It would be too easy for Chad Cartwright to talk himself into Nancy as the killer if she didn't intervene. She threw out another piece of information. "Do you know the Camerons, the couple that just opened the flower and gift shop?"

Cartwright nodded. "We've met. Nice couple. Good to see some people not collecting Social Security move into town for a change."

Lilliana bristled at the insult but decided to ignore it. "Well, there are rumors that Geoff Cameron had an affair with Fox Fordyce. Supposedly it was over by the Fourth of July. If it was, he might be a suspect. You know, a lover scorned and all that. If it wasn't, there's always the jealous wife." She paused to see how Cartwright reacted to that piece of information.

He narrowed his eyes. "Where did you hear that?"

"The information's out there," she said, quoting a line from Robert B. Parker's Jesse Stone novels. She decided to omit the follow-on line. "Ask around town. I'm sure someone must have known about it. You might find someone who can confirm whether the affair was ongoing or not." He looked interested, so Lilliana pushed a bit. "I'm still a stranger, so town people won't necessarily tell me everything. But you're a native, a hometown boy. I bet they'd be willing to tell you things they'd never mention to me."

"I still wish you'd tell me your source, Mrs. Wentworth. It would cut down on my investigation time."

"I'm sure you'll do fine." Having deflected the chief's suspicions away from Nancy, she thought it was time to go. "Let me know what you find out."

"And you do the same," he called after her, his words more of an order than a request.

It came to Lilliana as she plodded through the late morning heat that she hadn't been entirely honest with Chief Cartwright. It came to her that she'd made no mention of Christopher at all. She hadn't asked him if he knew MacAlistair had been living with Fox Fordyce, had had some kind of relationship with her. It was her civic duty to report that to the police. But only if she was sure there was a reason, she told herself. Christopher had explained that. *He had.* But if she was so certain, why did she need to convince herself? *Because he'd lied about his reason for speaking with the funeral director.* She couldn't help her doubts from niggling at the back of her mind.

CHAPTER TWENTY-ONE

The unfinished clay pot Lilliana picked up from the top of one of the shelves looked more lopsided than she remembered. The clay felt dry, so at least she'd be able to paint it during this class. She carried it over to her spot next to Pieter.

Her eyes widened as she saw that Pieter had not one, but three pots in front of him, with an assortment of paints in tiny paper cups—the kind you get at McDonalds to pump ketchup into—in an arc around the sheet of newspaper on which his creations sat.

"Good morning, Pieter. How did you ever make three pots?"

He smiled shyly at her. "I asked Grace if I could make more during the week. When she said yes, I came back to the craft room a couple of afternoons and made these two." He pointed toward two pots which were more elaborate than the first one he'd created during class. One had handles attached and the other had a bas-relief image on one side. Lilliana examined it more closely and saw it was a spray of flowers.

"You really do good work," she said. She looked at her own pot, with one eye squeezed tight and the opposite eyebrow arched skeptically. "Unlike me. This must be one of the worst pots ever coiled and scraped."

Pieter looked toward her effort. "You obviously haven't seen Harlan's or Bob's yet."

Lilliana turned slightly in her chair and tried to take a discreet look at the men's pottery. Pieter was right. Both of their projects were more lopsided than hers. Of course, Harlan had an excuse. He had Parkinson's, and his hands weren't steady enough to do this kind of work. Bob's poor performance, on the other hand, was probably due more to lack of interest than lack of ability. Sarah had tried to get him interested in several activities at the retirement community, but like a lot of retired men, he preferred to sit in front of the television watching reruns of programs from his younger years.

"Good morning, everyone."

She hadn't noticed the instructor entering the craft room, but she must have come in while Lilliana was chatting with Pieter.

"I see most of you have gotten your pots. They should be ready to decorate by now. You might want to test the bottom gently with your finger. If it's still soft, you'll need to let the pot dry further before painting it. You might try turning it upside down and coming back in a few days," Grace said.

Willie came into the craft room and apologized for being late before lumbering over to an empty chair. Meanwhile, Nancy was tapping the bottom of her pot with a doubtful look on her face. She tapped a little harder, and her finger broke through the soft clay. Nancy looked like she was going to cry.

Grace intervened with a smile. "Those things happen, Mrs. Gardner. It looks like instead of painting today, you'll be making a new pot."

"Could I?" Nancy asked.

"Certainly," Grace said. "I was just about to say that, if your pot isn't ready for painting today, you can come back during the week. Pieter has volunteered to help anyone who would like to come in between classes. You can arrange a time with him.

"For those of you who will be painting today, you can use these cups,"—she held up a stack of the same ones Pieter was using—"and pump some paint into them from the large jars I have here." Grace pointed toward a row of plastic paint jars that each had one of those pump devices attached to the lid, just as if they were filled with ketchup or mustard. "You don't need very much to decorate your pots, so it's better to take less rather than more."

Lilliana could imagine the kind of mess some neophytes made by taking too much paint and slathering it on too thickly.

"Also take at least one of these brushes to paint with," Grace said. "And fill a large paper cup with water so you can wash out your brush between colors. Any questions?"

When there weren't any, she said, "I'll be around to help you if you need it." Her voice had a note of finality to it, indicating the instructions to the class were over. Chairs scraped across the floor as most of the class headed to form a line in front of the paint jars. Willie went to retrieve his pot. Mary thumped over to Pieter to arrange a time during the week when she could come back and see if her pot was dry enough to paint.

Lilliana waited until the crowd around the paint thinned, then got up to choose her colors. She picked a turquoise and a dark red, thinking they'd show up nicely against the pale clay with which she'd made her pot.

There was something relaxing about painting designs on the clay, somewhat like the time she spent in her plant room repotting and grooming her African violets. She started out anxious as to whether her pot would be pretty enough to put one of the sale plants in it, then decided she'd rather enjoy the creativity of painting without the worry. If it didn't turn out to be a masterpiece like Pieter's, she'd keep it for herself. Maybe she'd keep it for herself anyway.

Willie had picked orange and black paint and was busily wielding a large brush to paint a Halloween theme on his pot. He hadn't done a bad job with his, but seemed content to settle for a large picture of a pumpkin instead of something more refined.

"A little early for pumpkins, isn't it?" she asked.

Willie grinned at her. "I like Halloween. Always liked all the kids in their costumes coming for trick or treat. Besides, who doesn't love a holiday where the whole idea is to collect and eat a lot of candy?"

Lilliana, concerned that Willie might be putting on weight again, asked quietly, "How are your wafers tasting?"

"They're fine now. I ate like a bird yesterday. Must have been a bad batch," Willie said. He examined his design with a critical eye. "I think I'm going to get some green paint and try some vines around this pumpkin."

Finished with the turquoise, Lilliana put down her pot and swirled her brush in the cup of water. Pieter had finished painting his first pot and was working on the second one. "When do you think you might be able to sell those pots to me?"

He looked up from his work and pondered the question. "Well, the paint has to dry first. That takes a couple of days. Then the pots need to be fired in the kiln. Miss Dalton said we'd probably put them in next week. That takes several hours —sometimes more than a day. I don't think we're going to add a glaze for the class, but you might want one for the plants you're selling?"

The way he asked it, he implied the answer, so Lilliana nodded.

"Okay, a day to cool down, then put the glaze on, then a few more hours in the kiln." Pieter touched his index finger to each of the fingers on his other hand, as if counting something, as he stared into space. When he arrived at a figure, he directed his gaze at Lilliana, "I'm afraid it will be at least a week."

"That would be fine," she responded, although she had hoped it would be sooner.

* * *

"How did your second pot turn out?" Lilliana asked Nancy as she followed her out of the class.

Nancy literally gave her the cold shoulder, turning her back so swiftly she stumbled with the momentum. She hurried down the hall toward her apartment, almost running away from Lilliana.

Disturbed, Lilliana charged after her. "Nancy."

Nancy showed no indication she'd heard her calling her name. A few of the class members paused to see what was going on, but most headed for their apartments here on the second floor or toward the elevator to go downstairs.

"Nancy!" Lilliana said louder as she hustled after her friend.

Nancy stopped outside her door. Lilliana continued her trip down the hall until she was standing beside Nancy. "Is there something wrong?"

Nancy's face sagged. A tear trickled down her cheek.

"Why don't we go inside and talk about it," Lilliana suggested.

Nancy nodded and unlocked the door. She lived in one of the small studio apartments that consisted of a bathroom, a combined living area, and a tiny section optimistically labeled kitchenette on the floor plan, one that amounted to a small refrigerator and a counter on which to put a microwave. A small cabinet mounted overhead might barely hold a cup, a glass, and a dinner plate. Nancy hadn't folded up the convertible sofa in the living area today, which left only the bed to sit on.

"Oh!" Nancy exclaimed as she saw the bed. "Wait just a minute while I fix this."

"Let me help you, Nancy." She was afraid the woman would hurt herself, although Nancy probably did this every day. Or, since she hadn't done it today, maybe she didn't. Lilliana knew what it was like living alone. You tended to do things more for convenience than for show. Which reminded her... She probably ought to examine her own apartment with fresh eyes now that there was a strong chance she might have company of her own.

Once the major piece of furniture had been returned to something suitable for sitting on, the two women sat.

"Would you like some tea?" Nancy asked, then looked worried. "I'm not sure I have any. Let me go look." She started to rise from the sofa.

"Please don't bother," Lilliana said. "I'd rather you tell me what's wrong."

"Oh, Lilliana," Nancy wailed. "I've seen you with Christopher in the dining room. And at the movies. How could you?"

Of course. She'd been so worried about her own appearance with him, the gossip and teasing that was sure to follow, Lilliana had almost forgotten there were other women interested in Christopher. "I'm sorry, Nancy. I didn't mean to hurt you. I assure you, it wasn't intentional."

"But you knew I liked him."

"Yes, I knew. But I didn't see him taking a particular interest in you"—that sounded a little harsh, but Lilliana always believed in being truthful—"so when we started seeing one another in various places"—no sense in being too specific, Lilliana thought—"it didn't occur to me that I was trespassing on your territory."

"Do you really like him?" Nancy asked.

What was that about being truthful? She almost regretted that in herself. Almost. Instead she nodded. "Yes, I'm afraid I do."

"And he likes you." Not a question this time.

Lilliana nodded again.

Nancy sat quietly for a moment weighing this information. "What about Pieter?"

Lilliana smothered a laugh. "I don't think he's involved with anyone."

"But do you like him, too?" Nancy asked.

"As a friend," she said. "Not in the way you mean."

"Do you think he might like me?" She looked anxious, as if afraid of more rejection.

"I think he's available." Not a direct answer, but she wanted to deflect Nancy from thinking about Christopher. "Why don't you see if he'll help you with painting your pot this week?"

"Grace did say he was willing to do that, didn't she?"

"She definitely said that. And I know for a fact Pieter will be spending extra time in the craft room working on his pottery."

"I'm going to ask him," Nancy said with confidence.

"That sounds like a plan to me." Lilliana smiled.

Crisis averted.

CHAPTER TWENTY-TWO

After her conversation with Nancy on their way out of the pottery class, Lilliana hurried back to her apartment. Nancy had gone off to find Pieter so she could set up a time to meet him in the craft room.

The components for the fairy garden were still sitting untouched in their bags in her plant room. Her arrangement with Esmeralda would do no good unless she put the completed garden on her patio. The small plants she'd bought were already wilting from lack of sun and water, and she scolded herself for forgetting about them.

After she placed the dish-shaped container on her work table, she gazed at it as she planned. She supposed her African violet soil would do, as long as she put a layer of marbles in the bottom for drainage and used a fertilizer more suited for foliage than blossoms. Her hands began the actions with the thought, grabbing the container of marbles from the shelf underneath the bench and putting several handfuls inside to form the lower layer. She then added a layer of soil over the top, being careful not to pack it down.

The plants had revived a little since she'd given them a bit of water before starting. It always amazed her how resilient young life was. Once she'd put the plants in their places in the soil, she carried the dish to the patio and placed it on the table, then went back for the bag containing the house, bench, bridge, and mailbox. When she returned, Bernadine was standing at the edge of the patio looking at her new addition.

"Good afternoon," Lilliana greeted her.

"Watcha got there?" Bernadine leaned over and peered at the garden.

It was no use lying to try to hide what it was called. Since the Camerons had displayed them at the Fourth of July celebration, someone was bound to know what a fairy garden was. Being caught in the omission would only draw more attention to what she hoped would be an unremarkable decoration on her patio. "It's called a fairy garden. I thought it would be kind of cute to have one with the miniature pieces and all." She illustrated by pulling the house out of the bag and holding it up so Bernadine could see.

"Where'd you get it?"

"At the Camerons' new shop," Lilliana said, then had a terrible thought. "Are you thinking of getting one?"

If other residents set out fairy gardens on their patios and balconies, Uaine might get confused and go to the wrong one.

"Let me see what it looks like after you set yours up."

Since she had the house in her hand, and as it was the largest piece, Lilliana decided to find a spot for it first. "I think I'll put the cottage beside the tree." She suited the action to her words by settling it next to the miniature boxwood on one side of the dish. Then she traced a path in the soil with two fingers. "The ground cover will spread over the soil, but I want this part to remain clear."

She pulled the bridge out next and put it at the end of the path she'd traced, then extended the path on the other side. "I'll have to figure out something that will look like a stream running under the bridge." She set the bench alongside the path.

"Looks like you could use more stuff," Bernadine said.

"Perhaps. I want to see how the plants grow first."

"Did it cost much for all that?"

"Not a whole lot. The dish and the cottage were the most expensive. The plants cost hardly anything at all."

Bernadine took her eyes off the garden and turned them toward Lilliana. "Do you think fairies will really come to a fairy garden?"

Now it was definitely time for a lie. Odd that the lie would be more believable than the truth. "Fairies aren't real, you know."

"Are you sure about that? My granny used to tell tales about the wee folk."

"Have you ever seen a fairy?" Lilliana temporized.

"Not personally, no. But I'd like to." Bernadine looked wistful. "I always thought it would be nice to have a fairy to grant you wishes."

Lilliana thought she had fairies mixed up with genies. "It would, wouldn't it?" She wondered how she could get Bernadine to move along. Or at least change the topic.

Fortunately, Bernadine had somewhere else to be.

"Well, it's almost time for bingo," Bernadine said. "See you later."

"Have a good time," she replied, relieved. Once she was sure Bernadine wasn't coming back, she pulled the mailbox from the bag, positioned it beside the cottage, and raised the flag.

The signal set, Lilliana had nothing to do until dinnertime. It was the perfect opportunity to read, but she'd finished the latest John Grisham legal thriller last night and hadn't yet picked out a new book. That was a problem easily remedied.

When she got to the library, she could hear the murmur of voices behind the closed door. Odd. The library door was supposed to remain open, unless there was something like the African Violet Club meeting going on. She ran her forefinger down the schedule taped to the door until she reached today's date. There was nothing on it for the entire day, much less this particular time. Lilliana rapped twice on the door and opened it, an apology ready in case she was interrupting something.

Chief Cartwright and Rebecca Cushing looked up at her from their seats at the library table. Cartwright's face was pinched tight over a clenched jaw. Rebecca nibbled her lip as her hands fidgeted in front of her.

"I'm busy in here, Mrs. Wentworth," the chief said.

"So I see," she responded dryly. "What's going on?"

"Oh, Lilliana," Rebecca began before Cartwright shot her an angry look.

"What is it, Rebecca?" It appeared as if Cartwright was bullying the old woman. That surprised her. He was usually considerate and sensitive to the residents of the retirement home.

"The chief thinks I gave Nancy my gun." Her voice trembled as she spoke.

Not asking for approval or waiting for an invitation, Lilliana sat next to Rebecca. "Let's see if we can straighten this out." She stared at the chief, daring him to tell her to leave.

He sighed and shuffled the papers in front of him. "Let's start from the beginning then. Tell me about the Fourth of July."

Rebecca looked at her for encouragement. Lilliana nodded.

"Well, like I told Lilliana, I saw Nancy Gardner follow Fox Fordyce behind the restrooms."

"Let's back up a bit," the chief said. "Did you and Mrs. Gardner go to the celebration together?"

"Why, yes, we did. We talked about it after lunch while we were sitting at the pool. Neither one of us wanted to go alone. We decided to walk over to the school together."

"Where did you meet?"

"Meet? We met a few weeks ago. Right here. At Rainbow Ranch."

The chief looked exasperated. "I mean where did you meet before going to the school?"

"Oh. Let me see…" Rebecca cupped her chin in her hand as she thought. "I know. Nancy said she wanted to take a shower and change before going. I didn't see the point in that. It was over a hundred degrees and would stay there until late at night. We'd just sweat like pigs walking down the hill, never mind up again."

"And?" the chief said.

"Oh. I told her I'd wait in my apartment, and she should come knock on my door when she was ready to go. I wanted to watch Jeopardy, you know." As if everyone watched Jeopardy in the afternoon. Of course, Lilliana did enjoy the quiz show herself. When she knew the answer to a question—or the question to an answer—it reassured her that she hadn't forgotten everything.

"So she came to your apartment…"

"That's right. I told her she'd have to wait until after Final Jeopardy." Rebecca nodded as if confirming to herself that's what had happened.

"Did Mrs. Gardner watch television with you?" the chief asked.

"I think she did. I really didn't watch her. I was too interested in the question and which contestant won."

"Did she stay in your living room or could she have gone into another room?"

"Well, come to think of it, she did say she was going to use my bathroom. It struck me funny, since she'd just come from her place. Why hadn't she used her own bathroom?"

The chief ignored the rhetorical question, but jumped on the content of her statement. "So Mrs. Gardner did have an opportunity to take your gun?"

Rebecca reddened and avoided the chief's eyes.

"Where did you keep the gun?" he asked.

"I used to keep it in the bedroom. In the drawer of my nightstand, you know, in case someone broke in while I was sleeping."

"And I assume the bathroom is near the bedroom?"

Rebecca licked her lips. "Yes, it is."

"So Mrs. Gardner could have easily gone into your bedroom and stolen your gun while you were watching the game show."

"Well, n-n-no," Rebecca stammered.

"What is it, Rebecca?" Lilliana asked.

"Well, you see, I *used to* keep it in the bedroom. But it disappeared about a month ago. I know because I opened the drawer to get my watch—I always kept it in the drawer when I wasn't wearing it—and I noticed that the gun wasn't there."

"Why didn't you report the gun as stolen?" Cartwright was angry now. "Don't you realize how important it is to report a stolen weapon?"

"Uh… I wasn't sure it *was* stolen. I thought I might have misplaced it." Rebecca was thoroughly embarrassed now. "I meant to look for it, but what with one thing and another, I forgot about it."

"Any other reason?" Lilliana prodded. She knew one thing the chief might not be aware of. When Rebecca appeared puzzled, Lilliana said, "Weren't you afraid to report it because then the retirement home would find out you had a gun?"

Rebecca nodded.

"Let me guess," the chief said. "Residents aren't allowed to own guns."

"No, they're not," Lilliana said. "I checked on that when I found out one of the residents had night terrors due to PTSD. I wanted to make sure he didn't own a gun, couldn't use one when he was out of his head."

Chief Cartwright heaved a sigh. "Can you think of anyone who might have been in your apartment and had an opportunity to take the gun?"

"It was so long ago," Rebecca said. "My memory's not what it used to be. I don't have that much company, but I do like to invite people in sometimes. To talk to, you know. It gets lonesome, living alone."

"Think, Rebecca. Try to remember who might have visited around the time the gun disappeared," Lilliana said.

Rebecca sat quietly for several minutes, brow furrowed. Finally she said, "I'm sorry. It's just so hard to remember back that far. I'm sure there must have been a few others, but I can only recall having that nice Christopher MacAlistair over for coffee and cake one day. I thought we might start dating." She shot a look of anger mixed with hurt at Lilliana. "Until *you* stole him from me."

Lilliana sighed.

CHAPTER TWENTY-THREE

Lilliana wanted to be sure she was drinking her first cup of tea on her patio early the next morning. When she'd raised the flag on the mailbox in the fairy garden, it had been with the intention of using it as a test. After yesterday, she had something else in mind.

Despite the sun barely peeking above the horizon, she found Uaine sitting on the little bench in the fairy garden when she opened the patio door. "Good morning," she said, glancing around to see if any of the residents of the retirement home were out and about. None were.

Uaine leapt up and fluttered over to her. "What can I do for you, Lilliana?"

"You fairies seem to be able to get inside people's apartments without them knowing you've been there." She thought of how they left Willie the wafers that suppressed his appetite and how they'd returned a button she'd lost.

"We can," Uaine said with a mischievous smile.

"Do you think you might be able to look for something,

even if you're not exactly sure what it is?"

Uaine scratched her head as she tapped her foot. "How would we know what it was then?"

"Well, it might be a piece of paper," Lilliana said. She wasn't sure herself what it could be. Then she had an idea. "One thing would be a piece of paper. Then there might be something else that would explain why the person had the paper."

"Do you know what the piece of paper is?" Uaine asked.

"A death certificate." Lilliana almost held her breath as she waited for Uaine's reaction.

The fairy fluttered up in the air in alarm. "Who died?"

"I don't think you knew her," Lilliana said quickly, trying to alleviate the fairy's fears. "It was Fox Fordyce several days ago."

Uaine settled in the fairy garden again. "Oh, well that's different. We knew about her, but never actually met. What would be the other thing?"

"Something that explained why the person had a copy of the death certificate."

Uaine scratched her head again. "I think you need to talk to Tam Lin. I'm not very smart, but Tam Lin knows all kinds of things. Wait right here."

Before Lilliana could object, the fairy darted off toward the desert foothills. She fretted that if Tam Lin took too long in getting here, he might be spotted. After all, he was larger than the flower fairies.

She needn't have worried. Tam Lin sprang up before her moments after Uaine had left. Lilliana blinked. He couldn't possibly have walked all that way. Or flown. He must have used magic.

"Uaine says you have a task for me."

"That's right," she said. "I'm afraid I'm not quite sure how to describe it."

Tam Lin did a little dance step. "Just do your best."

"There's a man who lives here—Christopher MacAlistair—who might have a copy of Fox Fordyce's death certificate. You know about that?"

"Sure and I do," Tam Lin said.

"He lives in the end casita." Lilliana pointed in that direction.

"Ah! The one with the beautiful music," Tam Lin said.

"Yes," she agreed. "That's the one. I'd like to know why he needs a copy of her death certificate. I don't have any idea myself, but I was thinking there must be something in his apartment that would give me a clue. Only I can't search it myself."

"So ye want me to search it for you," Tam Lin said. His eyes twinkled at the prospect. "Kind of like a private investigator."

"I was thinking more in terms of the Baker Street Irregulars," Lilliana said, naming Sherlock Holmes' crew of urchins, "but that's the idea. If you find the death certificate, there might be something with it that would explain why Mr. MacAlistair needs a copy."

"Aye, there might. When do ye need this by?"

Lilliana hadn't thought that far ahead. "Why, I suppose the sooner, the better."

"All right, then. I'll be back tomorrow." Tam Lin didn't wait for a response, but winked out of sight so fast Lilliana had no idea how or where he'd gone.

* * *

"You're awfully quiet this morning," Christopher said a few of days later. "Are you feeling well?"

They were walking down the driveway toward town after breakfast. Lilliana had mentioned she was going to bring more African violets to the Camerons, and Christopher had offered to help her carry them. She'd almost told him she didn't want him to come, but then thought that might be suspicious. She didn't quite trust herself to say much for fear of disclosing her doubts to him. "I'm fine. I'm just preoccupied."

"With African violets? Sounds like a serious hobby. Hobbies are supposed to be fun."

"Well, with that, but also with Fox Fordyce's murder."

Christopher raised his eyebrows. "The murder? Why would you be interested in that?"

They stopped to look for traffic on Main Street which, as usual, was non-existent, before crossing. That gave her a few more seconds to frame her thoughts. "Our Chief of Police isn't an expert homicide detective. He tends to jump at the first suspect and work to prove he or she is the murderer."

"And who might that be?" Christopher asked.

Did he look concerned?

"First it was Nancy, you know, because she was standing over the body. I think he still might suspect her."

"Since you said first, there must be a second," Christopher said. "And a third?"

"Just a second," Lilliana said. "Yesterday he was questioning Rebecca Cushing."

"Rebecca?" Christopher asked incredulously.

Then Lilliana remembered he didn't know the murder weapon was registered to Rebecca. *Or did he?* She wondered if he'd react to the knowledge about the gun. He also didn't know that she knew he'd visited Rebecca alone; at least she hoped no one had mentioned that to him. They'd reached the door of the flower shop. Lilliana paused with her hand on the doorknob. "Rebecca Cushing is the registered owner of the murder weapon."

She waited the length of a heartbeat. Christopher's lips parted just a bit, as if he were about to say something, but in the end he spoke no words. She opened the door and went in.

Penny Cameron looked up at the tinkle of the bell. "Good morning, Lilliana, Mr. MacAlistair."

"Good morning, Penny," Lilliana said.

Christopher lifted the basket up on the counter, and Lilliana took the plants out one at a time as she spoke. She'd brought three, repotted in Pieter's lovely handmade pots. "Since you mentioned last time that the African violets might sell better if they were in pretty pots, I decided to bring you some."

Penny clapped her hands. "Och, they *are* pretty!"

Lilliana was relieved. She'd been afraid Penny would be insulted that she hadn't bought the pots from her. "Of course, they'll have to cost a bit more."

"A lot more, I'd say. Wherever did you get these?" Penny asked.

"It turns out we have an expert potter at the retirement home. He's started to make pottery as a hobby and was perfectly willing to sell me these for my African violets."

They proceeded to negotiate a price for the potted plants

while Christopher took a walk around the store.

Penny pulled a ledger out from under the counter and opened it to a page that had Lilliana's name written at the top. "I'll just add these here," she said as she wrote a brief description of each plant with its price on lines beneath the first one that listed the original plants. "And I should pay you for the ones I sold." She opened the cash register drawer.

"Ones?" Lilliana asked. "Oh, that's right. You sold two."

"I've sold three," Penny said. "I was going to call you today and remind you to bring me more plants." She started counting out bills from the drawer into Lilliana's hand.

"That's wonderful." Perhaps her plan of making a little extra money would work out. She started to turn away.

"Wait a minute. You need to sign the receipt for me. I need records for the business, you know."

Lilliana did that and accepted her copy of the transaction from Penny. Christopher returned to her side. "Ready to go?" he asked.

She nodded.

As they made their way back to the retirement home, Christopher said, "Shall we have another practice session?"

"Practice session?"

"Surely you can't have forgotten. We still haven't picked a song for the talent show."

She had completely forgotten the talent show. She wasn't sure she could back out now. But until she was sure about Christopher, she didn't want to spend any more time alone with him. A weight settled in her chest. First she'd been afraid he was in love with Fox and that he was just toying with her.

Now she was afraid he was a murderer. It seemed in her case *the course of true love never did run smooth.* "A Midsummer Night's Dream," she mentally annotated.

"Lilliana?"

"Sorry, Chris. I was thinking about all I have to do today. I especially need to do laundry. And I should start some more plants since Penny appears to be selling them for me."

"After dinner then?"

"I'm rather tired already, and I was looking forward to a quiet evening of reading. Perhaps tomorrow." Internally she cringed at the half truth.

She was grateful when he didn't press her further.

CHAPTER TWENTY-FOUR

Despite ten hours of sleep, Lilliana yawned widely as, once again, she made an early arrival on her patio. She was having trouble keeping her eyes open. It turned out she wasn't telling a half truth when she'd begged off seeing Christopher last night because of fatigue. She hadn't read very long at all before closing her eyes and going to sleep. Carrying around the weight of her heavy heart must be wearing her out.

She'd struggled to get out of bed this morning, but she didn't want to miss Tam Lin should he return with information for her. She didn't have to wait long. She'd barely drunk a third of her tea when he popped up on the table beside the fairy garden.

"Good morning, Mrs. Wentworth. I'm back."

"Please call me Lilliana," she said, wondering why Tam Lin felt it was necessary to state the obvious. "Do you have something for me?"

"That I do." Tam Lin waved his hand and a document in a plastic sleeve dropped in her lap.

"What's this?" she asked, picking it up. It wasn't necessary for him to answer, since the words Whole Life Insurance Policy were plainly printed on the outside. She withdrew the pages from the plastic and unfolded them to read. Her throat tightened as she saw who the policy was for. She gasped when she saw the amount. Christopher MacAlistair was named as the beneficiary of a two hundred and fifty thousand dollar life insurance policy. The insured was Fox Fordyce.

Lilliana read the page slowly, confirming her first impression of the terms of the policy. She flipped through to the second and third pages, running her finger down the fine print and legalese that described what Christopher was entitled to, under what conditions, and one extremely salient fact. The beneficiary must present a copy of the death certificate for the insured in order to make a claim.

It was clear now why Christopher had asked the funeral director for a copy of the death certificate. Why in the world had Fox Fordyce had such a large policy? Clearly, a quarter million dollars was a strong motive for murder. Perhaps she had been thinking of changing the beneficiary after their falling out, and Christopher was pushed into acting so he could collect. *Was Christopher really that type of person?*

And if he was, why had she not seen it? Was she as bad as Nancy and Rebecca, bedazzled by his extraordinary good looks and sexy voice? Tears welled up in her eyes, and she felt as if a fist was clutching her heart.

"Thank you, Tam Lin." She didn't feel thankful. She felt betrayed. And foolish.

Tam Lin bowed. "Let Uaine know if you need anything

else." With that, the fairy disappeared as quickly as he'd come.

Now that she had the information, what was she going to do with it? It wasn't exactly proof, she told herself. At most it was circumstantial evidence. A motive. He'd had an opportunity to steal Rebecca's gun. And, she reminded herself, he hadn't been with her the whole time at the Fourth of July celebration. But there was no smoking gun. No one had seen him shoot Fox Fordyce. His fingerprints weren't on the murder weapon, she rationalized. Most of all, she didn't want to believe Christopher MacAlistair was a murderer.

* * *

Having been up at daybreak to meet with Tam Lin, Lilliana arrived early for breakfast in the dining room. They hadn't unlocked the doors yet, but even so, a line of those eager to eat extended down the hall. As she had hoped, Willie was near the front of the line, leaning on his walking stick. She caught up to him at the buffet.

"Willie, would you mind if I sat with you this morning?" she asked.

"Why do you think you have to ask?" Willie said. "You're always welcome at my table. Besides, it's nice to know you aren't ignoring me any more." His white teeth blazed out against his dark skin as he smiled, deflecting the hurt she knew he must be feeling.

"I didn't mean to ignore you," she said.

He patted her arm. "Don't take me so seriously. I think you make a handsome couple, you and MacAlistair."

Lilliana didn't dare meet his eyes.

They pushed their trays along the shelf that ran alongside

the steam table filled with food, filling their plates with scrambled eggs, sausage, and toast. Lilliana helped herself to coffee for a change. She felt this conversation demanded something darker than Earl Grey tea.

Willie chose a place near the window, somehow intuiting she wanted a private conversation. He lifted his plate and a large glass of orange juice from his tray and put them on the small table. Lilliana followed suit, then took the empty trays to a carrier nearby. Once seated in her chair, she spread strawberry jam on an English muffin. Willie had already finished half a sausage and a large chunk of his eggs.

"What's new?" Willie asked.

"You know I've been looking into the murder of Fox Fordyce."

"I thought you were, and Rebecca told me you helped her with young Cartwright the other day."

Lilliana nodded. "Yes. She's intimidated so easily, just as Nancy is. I don't think either woman could have killed Fox."

"I agree with you there," Willie said. "Do you want me to have a talk with the chief? Nothing official, mind you. Just to suggest that he might look a little further afield for his killer."

Lilliana hadn't thought of that before. "Perhaps."

She took another sip of her coffee. The acid churned in her stomach. "I wanted to ask you a question."

"What would that be?" Willie held the last bite of sausage on his fork, waiting for her answer.

"What would you do if you found out a person had a motive to kill someone? A very strong motive? But you didn't have any real evidence that he was guilty." The acid rose in her throat, and she reached for her water glass, hoping to put out the fire.

"So there's no forensic evidence, no fingerprints, no witnesses?" Willie asked.

She shook her head. "I'm afraid all the evidence is only what the chief discovered the first day. Nancy was holding the gun. Only her fingerprints were on it. The gun belongs to Rebecca, but she says it was stolen."

"It does? It was stolen?" Willie asked. His eyes narrowed as he contemplated this new-to-him piece of evidence.

"Sorry. I forgot you didn't know that." Lilliana wondered if she should have disclosed that piece of information. But Willie wasn't a suspect, and he had been Chief Homicide Detective for the Tucson Police Department for a long time. That's why she was seeking his advice.

"Tell me about your suspect." Willie sliced off another piece of sausage.

She drank her coffee. "I've found evidence that he'll benefit from Ms. Fordyce's death," she began and then realized she couldn't tell Willie how she'd obtained the life insurance policy. She decided to leave out the specifics of how Christopher would benefit. "Rebecca told me he'd been in her apartment before she discovered her gun was missing. Since she doesn't know exactly when the gun disappeared, it's not certain that he took it. It doesn't sound like very much when I tell you, but I assure you, it's been worrying me quite a lot."

Willie finished chewing his sausage and swallowed. "As it should. From what you say, your suspect had a motive, and it's very possible he had means. What about opportunity?"

She realized she'd left that out of her story. Lilliana nodded.

"He was at the fireworks show."

"Can he account for his whereabouts for the whole time?"

"That's hard to say. He did go off by himself a couple of times, but I don't know that anyone saw him near the toilets any time close to when Fox went there. It's possible Chief Cartwright hasn't had time to question everyone who was at the fireworks yet, or if he has, if anyone would have noticed this person in particular. I'm sure the chief wouldn't think to ask about the suspect. I haven't told him about my suspicions. Because I'm not sure. Yet. Should I, Willie? Is there enough to go to the chief with?"

Willie rubbed the back of his neck. "It's hard to say, Lilliana. It certainly is enough to warrant further investigation."

"What would you do?"

"I think I'd engage the suspect in some casual conversation. See if I could draw him out about the night of the murder. Sometimes when people get to talking, they say more than they mean to. Is this someone you know well enough to do that?"

"I think so." *Of course she did.*

"Good morning." Christopher's voice startled her, as if he could read her mind. "You didn't take your walk this morning. I was looking for you, hoping I might join you."

Willie scrutinized the Scotsman as if evaluating him in a new light before glancing at Lilliana.

She avoided Willie's gaze and turned her attention to Christopher. "I decided to skip walking today. It's getting too hot even in the early morning."

"That it is," Christopher said as he put his breakfast at the place next to her. Oatmeal and a banana and black coffee.

Once he was settled, he proceeded to put sugar on his oatmeal.

Now was as good a time as ever to put Willie's suggestion into action. "I've been thinking, Christopher, that this morning might be a good time to practice."

He stopped peeling the banana to give her a wide smile, eyes sparkling. "I'd be happy to."

"Practice?" Willie asked, looking from one to the other.

"Lilliana has agreed to sing with me at the talent show," Christopher said.

"I didn't know you were a singer," Willie said to Lilliana.

"I'm not, really. But Christopher plays the piano beautifully, so I'm sure he can cover up my mistakes."

"Nonsense." Christopher finished peeling the banana and started slicing it into his cereal. "Lil has a lovely voice." He put the knife down and wiped his fingers on a napkin. "Are you going to take part in the talent show?" This last was directed at Willie, who looked surprised.

"Me?" Then a sly grin passed over his face. "I'd dance, but my hip hasn't healed all the way. Maybe I could do some magic tricks."

"Magic tricks?" Lilliana said.

"I used to be somewhat of an amateur magician," Willie replied. "I'm a little out of practice, but I think I still have the props somewhere in my apartment."

This talent show was revealing more about the residents of Rainbow Ranch than Lilliana would have expected. And, if today went as planned, it might also reveal a killer.

CHAPTER TWENTY-FIVE

Her heart was all a-flutter as she walked to Christopher's casita with him. She wasn't sure whether it was because of her romantic feelings or the fear of what she might discover on this visit. Probably a little of both. He slipped his hand over hers once they were outside. Despite the heat, his skin was dry. She thrilled at the feeling of his fingers curling around hers, a soft, intimate gesture, almost as intimate as if they were caressing her.

"Have you thought about what you'd like to sing?" he asked in a normal tone of voice, as if he had no idea what his touch did to her. Which he probably didn't.

She shook her head, as much to clear it of her fantasies as to answer him. "Perhaps a show tune would be best. We seem to both like them."

"That we do," Christopher said, "and they're good for singing in harmony."

He opened the door to his casita and headed for the piano. Lilliana followed, glancing at the print of Fox Fordyce on the wall with mild dismay. *Why had he bought that?* Was he still in love with her, even though he'd denied it? Surely their relationship must have been more than traveling companions for her to have left him so much money.

He opened the piano bench and started shuffling the sheet music inside. His hand emerged with two or three selections which he held up for her approval. "Will these do for a start?"

She could read the word "Carousel" on one of them, "South Pacific" on another, and "The Sound of Music" on the third. "Rogers and Hammerstein is always a good choice."

He closed the bench and put the scores on the music rack.

She had to force herself to sit on the bench beside him. Who would have thought that sitting on a piano bench could be such an intimate position?

He raised the lid from the keys. "Which would you like to start with?"

She suddenly realized that each of the musicals was, at its heart, a love story. Dangerous ground for a woman who wasn't sure she dared trust this man. She picked the one she thought was safest. "'The Sound of Music.' How about 'My Favorite Things'?"

He opened to the page without comment and began to play. Soon they were smiling as they sang the words, moving their heads in time to the music. It was difficult not to feel buoyed up by the three-quarter time of the waltz. Before too long, it wasn't only their heads that were swaying back and forth. Their bodies joined in the movement, the pendulum arcs getting wider and wider until they were almost falling over, laughter bubbling up between the words, until Christopher pulled his hands off the keys and Lilliana from the bench and waltzed her around the room as they sang louder and louder. They ended the dance with a flourish and a bow. And a pounding on the wall of the adjoining casita.

"Oops," Lilliana said. "We're disturbing your neighbor."

"He's a crabby old man," Christopher said. "Pay no attention."

"Just the same," Lilliana said as she headed back to the piano bench, "I think we should choose something a little less boisterous for our second number."

Christopher sat beside her. "If you insist."

He held up the sheet music from South Pacific. She nodded her approval, and he opened the book to "Younger Than Springtime." Which was how Lilliana felt when she was with Christopher. She felt as if she were emerging from a long black tunnel into the clear daylight of spring.

She'd entered that tunnel when Charles had his stroke, plodded along through the months when he laid in the hospital bed, barely recognizing her, a strong man made weak and helpless by the explosion of a blood vessel in his brain, hoping and praying he'd recover. Which he never did. Then the months of mourning, when daily living was too much of an effort, too hard to bear, and her dearest wish was to join Charles in the afterlife.

A few months ago, Frank, noticing her admiring one of his plants, had given it to her, promising her that the blooms would brighten her days. Which they had. Raising African violets had taken her mind off her sorrows, brought her out of herself to the point where she'd suggested they form a club, and lit the path toward the tunnel's exit. With Christopher, Lilliana had emerged into full sunlight, marveling at the wondrous colors and sounds and smells all around her.

He segued into "Some Enchanted Evening," his deep, rich voice telling the story of seeing someone for the first time and knowing she would be special to him. Her throat tightened on the final line, and she wondered if Christopher would be the one to hold onto her forever. His eyes said he might be. "Oh, Chris, what are we getting ourselves into?"

His hands, which had rested on the keys at the end of the song, now lifted and clasped hers between them. "Something verra good, I hope."

With all her heart, she wanted to believe him. But she still had doubts. She wanted to ask him about the insurance policy, but how do you ask someone about something you're not supposed to know about? Her eyes flicked to the print of Fox Fordyce on his wall. He turned to follow her gaze.

"Is that a problem?" he asked. "Because, if it is, I'll take it down. It's only a print you know."

Lilliana slid her hands out from his and walked over to the picture, her heart thudding. Because she'd noticed the light from the patio door reflecting off a portion of the print. A raised portion. As she got closer, her eyes confirmed what she'd been afraid was true.

This wasn't the print Christopher had bought in Benson. This was the original oil painting from Fox Fordyce's house.

She whirled to face him. "I have to go now."

She practically ran for the front door, fighting to hold herself together long enough to reach the safety of her apartment. As she hurried down the path, she heard the strains of "If I Loved You" playing behind her.

CHAPTER TWENTY-SIX

Patting her face with a towel, Lilliana wasn't sure if there was more moisture from the cold water she'd splashed on her cheeks or the tears that didn't want to stop. She breathed deeply, a ragged breath that caught on the spikes piercing her heart, tearing out the fabric of what-might-have-been and leaving a shapeless lump of worn-out shreds of nevermore in its place. Another deep breath, this one less ragged as the spikes lost their sharpness. One more, and then she'd make her plans.

She could no longer keep what she knew from Chief Cartwright. There was only one place the painting could have come from. One reason Christopher had taken it. Like the insurance policy, it was something of value. He was not the Prince Charming she'd hoped for, but a gigolo, an opportunist living off the wealth of women he wooed.

She'd best walk into town while it was merely hot, rather than the torrid fever of afternoon. She might miss lunch, but she doubted she'd be hungry today. Or tomorrow, for that matter.

"Good morning, Mrs. Wentworth," DeeDee greeted her. "The chief just got back from his meeting in Bisbee."

Lilliana hadn't known he'd had a meeting in Bisbee, but she was glad he was back from it. She rapped on his door, then opened it and entered his office. He was wiping a cotton handkerchief across his brow. Before he could get to his nose, a globule of sweat dripped from the end of it. He sneezed in response, barely getting the handkerchief over his nose in time. "Excuse me," he said as he wiped his nose. "Allergies."

"Bless you." She took her usual place in the chair in front of his desk. She started talking before she could lose her resolve. "I know who killed Fox Fordyce."

"So do I," the chief said.

"It's not Nancy Gardner," she replied firmly.

"Rebecca Cushing? I don't think—" he stopped as Lilliana cut him off.

"No. It wasn't Nancy Gardner, and it wasn't Rebecca Cushing." Her mouth had suddenly gone dry. She licked her lips. "Could I have some water, please?"

Cartwright buzzed DeeDee and asked her to bring in two bottles of water. Once those were delivered and they had each taken a drink, the chief said, "So if it wasn't either of those two, who do you think it was?"

"Christopher MacAlistair."

The chief's face screwed up.

"He's new," Lilliana explained. "He's only been at the retirement home about a month or so." When the chief still looked as if he had no idea who she was talking about, she added, "He's the one who waited for me on the night of the murder."

The chief's face cleared. "Oh, the handsome one with the accent."

Lilliana nodded.

"Why do you think he did it?"

"Did you know he came to Rainbow Ranch with Fox Fordyce?"

The chief's eyes widened. "He did?"

"Yes, he did. He lived with her for a while before he moved into a casita at the retirement home. They had some kind of falling out. I think it had something to do with the fact he wasn't paying any rent or contributing to expenses."

"From what I know, Ms. Fordyce didn't need the money from a boarder." His eyes narrowed. "He wasn't just a boarder, was he?"

Lilliana felt the heat rise in her cheeks, took another drink of water to cover her embarrassment. "I'm sure I don't know."

Before she could falter, she continued her recitation of the circumstantial evidence. "He was in Rebecca's apartment before her gun went missing. Rebecca seems to think he could have taken it." She opened her purse and took out the insurance policy and lay it on the desk so Cartwright could read it. "Then there's this."

Cartwright took his time going over the terms of the policy. His finger paused on the date it was taken out, then the beneficiary, and finally the death benefit. He whistled through his teeth. "Where did you get this?"

This was the difficult part. She'd carefully planned her

response to the not unexpected question. "It came into my possession via a third party."

"Who?" he barked.

"I'd rather not say. Let's just say an acquaintance of mine noticed it and thought I should have it."

"You mean he stole it." Cartwright stroked his chin. "Not the best of evidence to present at trial."

"But you could use it?"

"I think so. I'll have to get in touch with the County Prosecutor."

"There's one more thing," Lilliana said. She told him about the print Christopher had bought and how it had been replaced by the original painting. "There's only one place he could have gotten that. He must have broken into Ms. Fordyce's house and gone to retrieve the painting after her death."

"Why would he have done that?"

"I think he formed an attachment to it when he lived with her." *And possibly to the subject?* "It's also worth a lot of money."

The chief leaned back in his chair and stared at a spot over her shoulder, evaluating the evidence she'd brought him. As if coming to a decision, he leaned forward as his eyes met hers. "Mrs. Wentworth, it appears you've solved another murder."

* * *

It was with great trepidation that Lilliana headed for the dining room that evening. If she'd had anything to eat in her kitchen, she would have skipped dinner. But she'd already missed lunch, and her stomach had been growling an hour before mealtime.

She'd ignored the ringing of her cell phone, the special tone for text messages, and anything else that might have led to contact with Christopher. Happily, she ran into Sarah and Bob Higgins as they came out of the elevator and joined them. She kept her head down and her eyes focused ahead of her to avoid seeing MacAlistair should he be anywhere nearby as they stuttered their way down the buffet line filling their trays.

"When do you think we should have the next club meeting?" Sarah asked as they made their way to a table.

So far, the African Violet Club had been meeting once a month. Lilliana wondered if that might be too often. "How does next month sound?"

Sarah looked disappointed. "So long?" She and Bob sat in adjoining chairs, their trays in front of them.

Lilliana sat next to Sarah once she'd arranged her meal on the table and taken the tray to the nearest stack. She realized Sarah looked forward to the meetings more than she did. Bob wasn't the greatest conversationalist, and Sarah probably enjoyed getting out of her apartment. "Do you think we should change to a two week schedule?"

Sarah's face lit up. "I think that would be much better. People enjoy the meetings. I'll have to reserve the library with Beverly tomorrow."

"Did you have an idea for a topic?" Lilliana asked.

Frank arrived with his own tray and, much to her relief, placed his dishes on the table in front of the seat beside her. She was now barricaded between two of her friends should Christopher show up. Nancy followed behind Frank and joined them, sitting opposite Lilliana.

"Maybe Frank does," Sarah said.

Bob shoveled food into his mouth.

"Maybe Frank does what?" Frank asked.

"Have a topic for the meeting," Sarah said.

Frank, being the most expert grower in the club, often provided the discussion topic. "Perhaps we could talk about design. We didn't have a design category in our last show, but it might be something fun for our members to try."

"What's design mean?" Sarah asked.

"Well, most shows have a theme," Frank began. "That gives the show a name to advertise and suggests something visual. Since we're in Arizona, we could call our next show something like 'Violets of the West,' which would suggest cowboys and cattle and the desert and mountains. The design category is one which would be an arrangement, not only of African violets, but other objects that carry out the theme."

Sarah looked puzzled. Lilliana wasn't sure she understood what Frank meant herself. "Could you give us an example?"

Just as she finished speaking, Christopher arrived with his meal. Before she glanced away, she saw his confused look, which he quickly covered up with a smile. "Good evening, everyone. May I join you?"

"Of course," Nancy said eagerly, and shifted her chair slightly to make room for Christopher beside her.

"Think of it as a diorama," Frank said.

"Frank is explaining what a design is," Nancy said.

"For the next show," Sarah added.

Lilliana didn't say anything. She purposefully cut off a piece of chicken—a tiny piece—and put it in her mouth. The entree, which had tasted so delicious moments ago, had lost its flavor.

"Anyway," Frank continued, "you set it up as a scene, using

bits of plants like bark and moss, as well as other material, to create a picture. Of course, you must have an African violet as part of it."

"That sounds like fun," Sarah said. The club president wasn't the best at growing the plants, and this might give her a chance to compete, thought Lilliana.

Just as she was about to force herself to speak, the dining room went quiet. The rattle of dishes and utensils and the murmur of conversation ceased as all heads turned in the direction of the entrance. Lilliana twisted in her chair to see what everyone was staring at. Her mouth fell open and her hand went to her throat, fingers fluttering as if trying to pull off the invisible noose tightening around it.

Her gaze followed Chief Cartwright as he strode toward their table and stopped behind Christopher's chair.

"Christopher MacAlistair, you're under arrest for the murder of Fox Fordyce."

Christopher's knife and fork clattered to his plate as he stared across the table at Lilliana, eyes wide, his complexion gone pale. His mouth opened, but no words came out before she averted her eyes from the hurt in his.

CHAPTER TWENTY-SEVEN

Lilliana carried two more African violets from the nearby lighted shelf to her potting bench. According to her label, these hadn't been repotted for over a year. More than time. If you didn't give the plants a fresh home, the soil tended to get compacted and the nutrients leeched out. It was also a good time to check for insects and, if needed, trim back the roots.

She'd spent most of the morning on this relatively mindless task, avoiding thinking of the events of last night. Avoiding thinking of Christopher and what might have been. It was easier to blank out her thoughts and focus on eliminating a long neck or a dead blossom or choosing mature leaves from which to start new plants.

Unfortunately, *Younger Than Springtime* had become an earworm, repeating itself over and over in her head. She'd even found herself humming it one time and had to force herself to stop. How was she going to replace the joy that spending time with Christopher had brought her? Going to lunch or the weekly movies with Nancy or Mary wasn't the same. Hardly the same. Christopher loved conversing about literature, was interested in art, and had reopened her heart and voice to music.

Stop it! she told herself. She'd misjudged the man, which just proved she was too old for romance. She should have known better. How many times had she shook her head at the foolishness of couples at the retirement home, comparing them to teenagers? Enough that she should have recognized the same symptoms in herself.

The last two plants were now happily repotted and ready to go back on the plant stand. She'd root the leaves later today. Adding water to the African violets had reminded her of the fairy garden sitting in the hot, dry air on her patio, and she thought she'd better water that before she forgot.

"About time you got here," Tam Lin complained as she stepped out of her air conditioned apartment into the hot, dry desert air of the patio. "I've been waiting forever."

Weighed down by sadness and wanting to avoid the stifling heat of July, Lilliana hadn't bothered with her customary cup of Earl Grey on the patio this morning. She quickly looked around for any prying eyes. Fortunately, the heat had kept everyone else indoors as well.

"You really need a bigger bench." Tam Lin shifted his bottom. Taller than the flower fairies like Uaine, his bent knees came close to his chin, and with his arms stretched out to either side, his hands dangled off the back of the bench.

"I'm sorry, your majesty," Lilliana said. "I didn't expect you to be waiting here." As if she needed to worry about a cranky fairy. With the watering can in her hand, she was tempted to go ahead with her task and, accidentally of course, give Tam Lin a shower in the process. It almost made her smile. Almost, but not quite.

Tam Lin leapt up and paced as he spoke. "I'm bored." He bent over and picked a leaf from one of the plants, sniffed at it, then threw it away. "I was wondering if you had another mission for me."

She shook her head. "No. I'm afraid you found what I needed. Not what I wanted, but what I needed." She sniffed as her eyes filled with tears.

"Oh, no! Did I do something wrong?" Tam Lin jumped to his feet. "Can I fix it?"

"It's not your fault," Lilliana said.

"But you're not happy. Can I get you something to make you happy? I'm good at that. Perhaps a crystal from the cave. Or a bird to come sing to you." He did a little dance step. "I'm not sure what you like, other than your African violets, of course. Now, that man you sent me to…"

Lilliana perked up. "What about him?"

"I didn't think I should take something from him without giving him something in return. I saw him looking at that picture on his wall. He seemed to like it well enough, but I remembered I'd seen one quite similar, only much nicer, somewhere else."

"Somewhere else?" There was only one place where Tam Lin could have seen the painting. "When were you in Fox Fordyce's house?"

Tam Lin shuffled his feet and averted his eyes. "Once or twice."

"Wait," she cried. "Are you saying you're the one who switched Christopher's print for the original painting?"

"Well, Miss Fox certainly wasn't going to look at it any more. It didn't take much effort on my part. Just a wee bit of magic, you know, and, clink, clank, clunk, they swapped places. Is there something like that I could get for you?"

Lilliana's head was spinning. She sank into her chair, dropping the watering can with a clatter as she did so, ignoring her wet feet as the water splashed out of it.

"Och, no!" Tam Lin hopped from one foot to the other, clearly agitated, before leaping into the air and fanning her face with the beating of his wings. "Shall I get Esmeralda?"

She started to shake her head, but the landscape tilted, so she forced herself to speak instead. "No. I'll be fine in a minute."

Christopher hadn't stolen the painting. He might have stolen the gun from Rebecca, but there was no evidence of that. Maybe he hadn't murdered Fox Fordyce after all. But there was still the life insurance policy. *Why hadn't she asked him about that?*

Because she didn't want to admit she knew about it.

"Lilliana?"

She'd forgotten Tam Lin was there. "It's all right, Tam Lin. You'd better get back to Fairyland before someone sees you."

"Are you sure?"

It looked as if she had more investigating to do. "I'm sure. I'll signal if I have anything else for you."

CHAPTER TWENTY-EIGHT

Later that day, after a meager breakfast of cheese and crackers, a succession of three quick taps sounded on Lilliana's door. Curious as to who would come visiting, she opened it to find Dan, the UPS driver, with a package for her.

He held out the box in one hand and the electronic pad in the other. "Please sign in the blank area, Mrs. Wentworth."

"What is it?" After signing her name in an ugly scrawl on the glass screen, she looked at the return address. "But I didn't order any African violets," she said, recognizing the name of a hybridizer she'd ordered from before.

"Maybe someone sent you a present," Dan said.

"Perhaps." She detached the packing slip from the carton and examined it. Heartache squeezed her chest at the thought that Christopher, her not-so-secret admirer, cared enough to buy her this thoughtful gift.

"Busy delivery day here. And a heavy one, too. These boxes,"—Dan pointed to the two-wheeler with three identical boxes stacked on it—"for Mr. Joncker weigh a ton."

"Oh, he must be getting his clay. Let me go with you." Glad for something to distract her from the reminder of what might have been, Lilliana put the box of African violets on the kitchen counter and grabbed her keys.

"Clay?" Dan asked as the walked down the hall together.

"Pieter's making pots for my African violets. He's quite good at it."

"I hope making pots doesn't become a popular hobby. I don't want to throw my back out again."

Lilliana was concerned, then realized Dan was joking. By this time, they'd reached Pieter's apartment, and Dan knocked on the door with the same distinctive three quick taps as he'd used on Lilliana's. It took a few minutes before Pieter opened it. When he did, his eyes widened at the sight of her, then quickly darted to Dan.

"I have three boxes for you," Dan said. "Mrs. Wentworth tells me you're a potter."

"Ah! Yah, I like to make pottery. I didn't expect the clay would come so fast. Come in, come in." Pieter stood back and opened the door so Dan could roll the two-wheeler inside.

"Where do you want it?"

Pieter looked over his shoulder, then said, "Put it in the living room, please." He led the way down the short hall, then gestured toward the half wall that separated the tiny kitchen from the living area. From what Lilliana could see, Pieter had a small one-bedroom apartment identical to Sarah's.

After unloading the cartons, Dan presented Pieter with the electronic pad to sign. "Take care, Mr. Joncker. Don't hurt yourself carrying those cartons," he said on his way out.

"I wonder how heavy they are." Pieter grasped the top one and gave it a test lift of a couple of inches. "Not too bad. I hope I can carry it all the way to the craft room."

"Maybe you should have asked Dan to bring them up there."

"No. I'd be afraid someone else would use my clay. I'll take the boxes up one at a time." That decided, Pieter turned to Lilliana. "Was there something you wanted?"

"Penny Cameron told me she was sure the African violets in your beautiful pots would sell quickly. When Dan told me he was delivering your clay, I wondered how soon you could have more pots ready for me."

Pieter scratched his chin. "I could start tomorrow, I think. Perhaps next week I could have a half dozen pots for you."

"So long?" Lilliana had hoped he could make them faster.

"Yah. The drying takes time. The firing takes time. You can't do it any faster or you'll ruin the pots. Haste makes waste as my Anna used to say." His eyes filled with sadness.

"It's hard to lose a spouse," Lilliana said, thinking back to Charles.

"Yah." Pieter walked over to an end table beside the sofa and picked up a picture. Lilliana followed, and when she joined him, he held the photo so she could see it. A woman with gray hair and one of the warmest smiles she'd ever seen stared out from the frame. The woman was the perfect image of a Midwestern farmer's wife.

"My Anna," Pieter said by way of explanation. "We got married right out of high school, and she came to live with me on my family's dairy farm."

"Where was that?" Lilliana asked, not remembering what she

was sure she'd heard at one time.

"Wisconsin. My boys run the dairy farm now." He gave her a weak smile. "Wisconsin winters are too cold for these old bones."

"She never lived here, did she?" Lilliana couldn't remember ever seeing her at the retirement home. Of course, she hadn't been aware of the other residents until recently, but she was sure she would have noticed Anna.

"No. She didn't live long enough to retire. Life is hard for a woman, and Anna always insisted on helping with the livestock." His lower lip started to tremble. "There was an ice storm. Anna had been coughing for days, but she didn't want us to lose any animals. Out so long in that weather... She got pneumonia and died."

"I'm so sorry," Lilliana said. No wonder Pieter had moved to Arizona. She imagined the memories were too poignant in Wisconsin.

"Anyway, we go on, don't we?" Pieter asked.

"Yes, we do."

* * *

Jaclyn was already seated at a booth near the back of Cathy's Café when Lilliana entered. The owner of Pulaski's Gourmet Grocery had called her to ask about her welfare since Lilliana hadn't been into the store recently. After reassuring Ted's great-granddaughter that she was fine, Jaclyn had told her about a new shipment of chocolates that had arrived. Feeling guilty for neglecting her, Lilliana had suggested lunch together.

"How are you doing?" Jaclyn asked once Lilliana was seated across from her.

"I'm fine, just like I told you over the phone. I have the constitution of a grizzly bear." Lilliana smiled to reassure her.

"But not the temperament, I hope." Jaclyn smiled in return, then her face turned serious. "I heard about Christopher MacAlistair."

"Oh, that." She picked up her napkin from the table, unfolded it, and put it in her lap, busied herself with pleating and unpleating the paper until it started to shred.

"Yes, that."

Cathy came over and took their orders, saving Lilliana from any immediate discussion of Christopher's arrest.

"He didn't strike me as a murderer," Jaclyn said. "In fact, quite the opposite."

"I know." The words came out in a whisper that choked off at the end. She swallowed hard, trying to loosen the tightness in her throat. "It just goes to show you, you can't trust first impressions."

An awkward pause stretched between them. The restaurant filled up with customers as the noon hour approached. It wasn't usually this crowded.

"How are your African violets doing?" Jaclyn asked.

Lilliana brightened at the change of topic, smothered the image of the new box of plants sent by Christopher before it could dampen her mood. "They're doing wonderfully. In fact, I just repotted a whole shelf-full this morning. Buying those lighted plant stands was a very good idea."

"Mind if I join you?" Sam Horn's voice said from the aisle. "All the tables seem to be taken today."

Jaclyn slid over in the booth to make room. "Not at all. Any idea what's going on?" She waved at the full tables.

Cathy dropped off the women's meals and took Sam's lunch order. Lilliana's enchilada with the sauce and melted cheese looked delicious, and the portions of refried beans and rice that accompanied it were large enough for a second meal. Jaclyn picked up a triangle of her turkey club sandwich. Apparently she'd decided on a change from her customary hamburger and fries.

"The realtor is doing an open house on Fox Fordyce's place," Sam said, as if that explained everything.

"Ah. The ghouls want to see where the murder victim lived." Lilliana ate some of her enchilada.

Sam nodded. "Most likely."

"We were just talking about Lilliana's African violets," Jaclyn said. "Penny told me she was selling them in her store."

"Mrs. Cameron was kind enough to take a few plants on consignment. I wonder if some of these people might find their way down there and buy some."

"That would be wonderful," Jaclyn said. "Are they selling well?"

"Much to my surprise, yes. I think they'll sell better now that Pieter Joncker is making pots for them."

"Pieter Joncker?" Jaclyn asked. "That's a name I haven't heard in a while. How do you know him?"

"He's a member of the African Violet Club," Lilliana said. "It turns out he's also a talented pottery maker."

"I didn't know he lived at the retirement community," Jaclyn said. "I thought he would have left Arizona by now."

"You know him?" Lilliana had started to lift a forkful of rice to her mouth, but now stopped it in mid-air.

"Of course. He bought Ms. Fordyce's cattle ranch when she sold it after her rodeo career." Jaclyn had finished the quarter sandwich she'd started on and picked up the next piece. "He used to ask my Grandpa Ted for advice."

"He did?" Lilliana had discovered small town syndrome once again. Having spent most of her life in cities, she wasn't used to the idea that in small towns everyone knew everyone else.

"All the time. He was a dairy farmer in Wisconsin and thought raising cattle in Arizona wouldn't be all that different." Jaclyn bit into her sandwich, chewed, and swallowed. "Needless to say, he was wrong."

Cathy brought Sam a plate of the meatloaf special. "Anything else I can get you folks?"

"No, thanks," Lilliana said while Jaclyn and Sam shook their heads. "How long ago was this?"

Jaclyn stared into the distance as she searched her memory.

"It had to be at least seven or eight years ago," Sam said. "Before that big ice storm."

"That's right." Jaclyn's face cleared. "My great-grandfather still owned Rainbow Ranch then."

"Ice storm?" Lilliana asked. Pieter had mentioned an ice storm.

"Worst one in a hundred years," Sam said. "Coated everything in an inch of ice. Knocked out the power for a week in some places."

"It was so sad," Jaclyn said. "The Jonckers worked so hard to make a success of cattle ranching, but I don't think they were ever cut out for it."

Lilliana shifted her gaze to Sam as he spoke. "Poor Pieter. Anna was dead for two days before anyone knew."

"You're saying Anna got pneumonia and died on the ranch in Arizona?" Lilliana asked.

"That's right," Sam said.

"I thought Pieter was talking about the farm in Wisconsin when he told me about the ice storm." Lilliana's brain was busy rearranging the puzzle pieces in light of this new information. "What happened after that?"

"Well, Mr. Joncker's heart just wasn't into ranching," Jaclyn said. "And then there was the drought."

Lilliana knew all about the drought. Ted, Jaclyn's great-grandfather, had told her that was what had forced him to sell his ranch to the developers who built the retirement home. "What about the drought?"

Sam picked up the story. "The ice storm was a fluke. An aberration in the middle of a number of years with no rain. Like a lot of other ranchers, Pieter lost most of his cattle. Without cattle to sell, he wound up with a ton of debt. Bank foreclosed on the ranch a couple of years after that."

"Not hungry, Mrs. Wentworth?" Cathy asked when she returned to their table, noting how Lilliana had left most of her food on her plate.

"I'm afraid not." Then, wanting to reassure the owner of the café, she added, "The food was delicious. Can I have a to-go box?"

"Sure 'nough." Cathy left to get the box.

"Is that when Pieter moved into the retirement home?" she

asked.

"I think so," Sam said. "It might have been built by then."

"I'd better get back to the store," Jaclyn said. "Should I put aside some of those chocolates for you?"

"Not too many," Lilliana said, but her mind wasn't on chocolates. It was on the visit she needed to make to Chief Cartwright.

CHAPTER TWENTY-NINE

The next day, Lilliana sat in the craft room, waiting, a mystery by Robert B. Parker in her lap. She'd brought it to pass the time, but she was too nervous to read. She'd overheard Pieter in the dining room at breakfast say he was going to spend the afternoon making more pots, so she'd hurried to be there right after lunch. Of course, afternoon could mean twelve-thirty or four o'clock. It was already after two.

She needn't have worried. The door to the craft room nudged open slowly as Pieter backed into it, a box of clay in his hands. He almost dropped the box when he saw her sitting there.

"Come to watch me make your pots?" he asked as he put the heavy carton on the table.

"Actually, I came to talk to you."

His bushy white eyebrows lifted. "About what?"

"About the ranch."

Pieter pried open the carton and lifted out a block of clay sealed in clear plastic packaging. "What ranch?"

"The ranch you bought from Fox Fordyce." Lilliana put her book on the table and leaned toward Pieter. "The ranch where you lost most of your savings when the drought hit. The ranch where your wife died in an ice storm."

Pieter's brow creased as his eyes darkened with anger. "She knew," he said darkly as he broke off a piece of clay from the block.

"Who knew?" Lilliana's heart tripped in her chest. *She needed to get him to say it.*

"Fox Fordyce," he growled. "She knew the drought wouldn't support enough cattle on the ranch to earn a living. She knew I knew nothing about raising beef cattle on an open range, that it wasn't anything like raising dairy cattle. She took advantage of my ignorance, told me how wonderful it was that someone like me wanted to buy the ranch."

He punched the lump of clay with his fists, grabbed it and kneaded it as if getting revenge on it.

"And then she came back to town," Lilliana prompted.

Pieter nodded. "She came back to town. Started talking about having the rodeo on the old ranch. Again she was going to make money from it, and I would have nothing."

"You couldn't stand the idea of that happening."

He slapped the clay hard. "Everyone treated her like a queen, like a celebrity. That big article in the paper, the television people. No one said anything about her taking everything from me. Including my Anna." Pieter sobbed.

Lilliana was afraid she was going to have to probe more directly, but now that Pieter had started speaking, she tried to be patient.

Pieter's face reddened. "I had to make her pay. I couldn't let her get away with it. So I shot her." His hands clenched into fists as he pressed his lips together.

"Where did you get the gun?" Lilliana asked. She wanted to tie up all the details.

"The gun?"

"The gun you shot her with. It wasn't yours, was it?" Miss Marple always got the killer to confess easily. As a matter of fact, they usually couldn't wait to tell her how they did it—if she hadn't figured it out long before. Lilliana was going to have to study Miss Marple's techniques more closely.

"No, it wasn't mine. Rebecca told me about the gun she kept in her nightstand, asked me if I thought they'd evict her if someone found out. It wasn't hard for me to get it when she was otherwise occupied."

"So you took Rebecca Cushing's pistol with the express purpose of killing Fox Fordyce."

"I did," Pieter said with resolve. Then a startled look came over his face as he realized what he'd done, quickly followed by clouds of anger. "You think you're clever, don't you? Getting me to confess, I mean. You probably think you can get in good with the police chief, get your boyfriend out of jail. Well, you're not going to have a chance to tell anyone."

Pieter lunged in her direction, hands outstretched, and wrapped them around her throat so tightly Lilliana didn't have a chance to scream. His thumbs dug into her windpipe as firmly as they'd dug into the clay.

She pushed at him with her hands as she tried to get a breath, but Pieter was too strong for her. She tried to kick him, but couldn't get enough leverage to put any strength behind the effort. Pieter loomed over her, heaving deep breaths as he strained to strangle her.

"Stop right there," Chief Cartwright's voice boomed from behind her.

Startled, Pieter loosened his grip just enough for Lilliana to escape his grasp. She rose to her feet, her chest heaving with the effort to draw air into her lungs. Cartwright stood in front of the open door to the closet, gun drawn and aimed at Pieter.

"You might have come out of the closet a little sooner," Lilliana said as she rubbed her neck.

"Sorry, Mrs. Wentworth. I wanted to make sure Mr. Joncker had said all he was going to." In his firmest tone, he addressed Pieter. "Pieter Joncker, you're under arrest for the murder of Fox Fordyce."

CHAPTER THIRTY

Lilliana waited nervously in the lobby of Town Hall, feeling an urge to chew on her fingernails. She tried pacing instead, but her legs felt wobbly, and she feared she might fall if she kept it up. Chief Cartwright had taken Pieter Joncker to the basement, where there were a couple of holding cells for keeping drunks overnight or prisoners destined for the county jail until they could be transported.

She hadn't realized Christopher was still there until the chief told her he'd be releasing him immediately. How could she explain the suspicions she'd had that led to his arrest? Would he forgive her? Or would he be angry? Justifiably so, of course. Lack of trust was the quickest way to kill a relationship.

A humming noise came from the direction of the elevator, and her heart pounded in her chest. When the annunciator chimed signaling the car's arrival, her head swam, plunging her consciousness to a location somewhere around her knees. She took a slow, deep breath. She could do this. She must do this, regardless of the outcome.

The elevator door opened, exposing a slightly disheveled Christopher MacAlistair, his hair ruffled, clothes wrinkled, and a layer of stubble on his face, so different from the elegantly groomed man she'd come to know. But when he smiled at her, he was the most handsome man she'd ever seen.

"Oh, Christopher, can you ever forgive me?"

His smile faltered, causing her heart to trip over the doubt he must feel. Glancing over at DeeDee behind the reception desk, he said, "Let's find a place to talk."

He took her hand and led her out of the building, then continued down Pulaski Street. Dark clouds accompanied by the rumble of thunder were rolling in from the mountains.

"It looks like it's going to rain," he said.

"Yes, it does." It was the best Lilliana could do under the circumstances. She wasn't sure whether to launch into her explanation or wait for him to ask. A cold wind blasted them as they emerged from the shelter of the side of Cathy's Café. Lightning flashed overhead; thunder assaulted their ears.

"We'd better hurry." He pulled her across Main Street, the wind whipping through their hair. Large drops of rain plopped on her face as she looked up at the sky, onyx black and angry. He hurried her up the drive as the drops became more frequent. The cold rain fell on her shoulders, splattered the legs of her pants. She shivered.

The building wasn't far now, but they'd have to hurry if they didn't want to be drenched by the storm. A stroke of lightning split the sky, blinded her. She stumbled, and Christopher caught her in his arms, steadied her, then pulled her toward the gazebo.

Just in time, as it turned out. The heavens opened, rain falling as if dumped from some celestial bucket. Pea-sized hail rattled on the roof of the gazebo as thunder shook the ground.

They sat inside the storm, huddled together. She took comfort from the fact that Christopher wrapped her in his arms. He couldn't be too angry if he was holding her, could he?

Like most desert thunderstorms, this one ebbed as quickly as it had swept in from the mountains, settled into a gentle rain that would most likely stop in a few minutes. As if realizing they didn't have much time before other residents might emerge from the retirement home, Christopher asked, "Lil? Cartwright confirmed he arrested me based on your suspicions. Why did you think I killed Fox?"

The moment she'd been dreading had finally come. Lilliana twisted in his arms, pulled back a bit so she could face him. "Your explanation of telling the funeral director about a burned out light bulb didn't quite make sense. When he told me the real reason you spoke to him was to ask for a copy of her death certificate, I had to find out why."

Christopher hung his head.

"Then I found out about the life insurance policy"—Lilliana suddenly realized she couldn't possibly tell him how she'd found out about it, and she dare not mention the painting for the same reason—"and it made sense. Unfortunately, what also made sense was that two-hundred-fifty-thousand dollars is a very strong motive to kill someone."

"I should have known you were too smart to believe my lie."

His eyes were still looking at the floor of the gazebo as he said this. He raised them to meet hers. "I'm sorry I lied to you, Lil. I thought you might not understand."

"I still don't," she said. The rain had stopped now, leaving the desert air fresh and cool and filled with the scent of creosote bushes. "Why did Fox Fordyce make you the beneficiary of her life insurance?"

His pulled his arms from around her, leaned back, folded them protectively across his chest. "On our way to Arizona, we stopped in Las Vegas for a few days. Not exactly on the way, but Fox's son works in a hospital in Henderson, and she wanted to see him. When we met for dinner one night, Fox had a vicious argument with her son. He never approved of her lifestyle, and when she told him she was traveling with a man from Scotland, someone she'd met at a bar, he became outraged and stormed out. He called her several times a day trying to persuade her to 'grow up.' As you can imagine, she didn't care for being scolded by her own son.

"After a night in the casinos filled with gambling and drinking, she decided she would get her revenge by changing the beneficiary on her life insurance. Since she didn't have any other relatives, and I was there, she decided to make me the beneficiary. At the time, I agreed with her."

He looked at Lilliana shamefacedly. "I must confess, I was also drinking that night and might not have been using my best judgment. She insisted we contact the insurance company right away, which she did."

"She didn't change it back after she threw you out?" Lilliana asked.

Christopher shook his head. "She still hadn't made her peace with her son, and I suppose she had the same problem as in Las Vegas. She didn't have anyone else to make beneficiary. And, I'm ashamed to admit, the idea of inheriting all that money was a great temptation.

"Traveling gets expensive, and I do like to travel. The money would allow me to keep my casita here and still continue to see the world."

Alarmed, she had to ask, "Are you planning on leaving?"

A gentle smile played across his face. "Not any time soon. Unless you want me to go."

Lilliana was quiet for a while as she reflected on what he'd told her. Though greed wasn't a positive character trait, she supposed no one was perfect. Not even herself. "No, I don't want you to go.

"I'm sorry I had you arrested. I should have asked you about the insurance before I went to the chief. But I was afraid you were one of those men who attach themselves to rich elderly women, hoping to take advantage of them for their money. Not that I have a lot of money, but you might have thought I did."

She hesitated before saying plainly the last thing on her mind, but now was not the time to hold back. There had been too much of that. "I thought you wanted me for money, not for love."

Christopher unfolded his arms, took her hands in his, and quoted in his marvelous rich voice:

"Doubt thou the stars are fire;
Doubt that the sun doth move;

Doubt truth to be a liar;
But never doubt I love."

Lilliana, recognizing the lines from Hamlet, laughed and asked, "Are you Hamlet or Polonius?"

Christopher laughed in return, a nervous laugh, before speaking. "Hamlet, I hope. And I hope you will be my Ophelia —without the madness or the dying." He smiled at her, an anxious, waiting kind of smile.

The sun was breaking through the clouds, but it was Christopher's words that made her heart leap. With reckless abandon, she replied, "I just might be mad already."

The worry left his face. "Then we shall be mad together."

CHAPTER THIRTY-ONE

For the first time in ages, Lilliana had put on both a dress and makeup. She peered into the mirror, trying to decide if she'd used too much eyeliner and mascara, if the lipstick shade she'd chosen was a tad too vibrant for a woman of her age, or the blush she'd brushed on her cheeks looked like clown makeup. She had no idea what kind of lighting they would have in the television room, and she knew how washed out a woman could look under bright lights. On the other hand, she didn't want to look like a hussy up close.

She backed away from the mirror for a different perspective, decided her face would do, and then began the same scrutiny of the dress. She'd chosen an electric blue cocktail dress, thinking to match her eyes, but the color was closer to Christopher's than her own. Lilliana's eyes were more of a cornflower blue, lighter and not half as arresting as his. The dress was very pretty, though, and well worth the extra expense.

Finally, with everything else in place, she reached up and

removed the band from the long gray tresses gathered at the back of her neck. In the heat of the summer, she generally kept her hair bound up, but tonight she wanted to wear it loose. She picked up her hairbrush and stroked the strands, coaxing them into gentle waves that flowed over her shoulders.

A knock on her door startled her, even though she was expecting it, and her heartbeat changed from a waltz to a tarantella. She put the brush down and went to answer it.

"Good evening, Lil."

Christopher was dressed in a charcoal gray suit, white shirt, and, as if he'd planned it, a tie of a color that matched her dress. He carried a soft-sided black travel tote. His beard and hair were freshly trimmed, and as he smiled at her, Lilliana thought he had to be the handsomest man in Rainbow Ranch.

"I'm ready. Let me get my purse." She hurried to the bedroom to retrieve it, then the two of them made their way to the common area of the retirement home.

The cacophony coming from the entrance to the television room told them the magnitude of the crowd before they were close enough to see it. Once they reached the doorway, the two of them paused, looking for a non-existent seat or two. Inside, it was standing room only, with people lined up along the walls at the back and to the side. Lilliana felt a swarm of butterflies take flight inside her. She hadn't expected this many people to show up for the talent show.

Mary stood at the door, a stack of programs in hand. She handed one to Lilliana.

"It looks like we'll have to stand," Christopher said unnecessarily. He sidled along the back wall until he found a space big enough for the two of them to occupy if they stood very close to one another. She had no problem with that.

A microphone and speakers were set up in front of the large television screen, and the portable spotlight that shone on it made Lilliana grateful she'd put on the makeup.

Russell Ellison, owner of the retirement community, stepped up to the mic. She was surprised to see him at the event. He was rarely there in the evening. "I'm glad to see such a terrific turnout tonight for our first annual talent show. I expect to discover we have many talented people in our community. Remember to applaud loudly for your favorites because prizes will be awarded based on your response."

Prizes? Lilliana hadn't realized this was a competition. Not that it mattered to her whether she won a prize or not. She only cared about winning prizes where her African violets were concerned.

"First up is Bernadine Meade, performing a song and dance number," Ellison announced. The audience responded with clapping and whistles as Bernadine made her way to the front of the room.

Christopher leaned over and whispered in her ear. "When do we perform?" When she didn't respond right away, he gestured toward the program in her hand.

"Oh." She'd forgotten all about the program. She scanned it quickly, then swallowed hard. "We're last." She wasn't sure she could bear the tension all the way through the show. Christopher dipped his head to indicate he'd heard her.

Bernadine stood in the spotlight, wearing a top hat and carrying a cane. She looked questioningly at Ellison, who nodded as a go-ahead signal. Bernadine cleared her throat, then, in a scratchy voice sang, "Dah dah da-da-da, dah dah da-da-da," the easily recognizable opening to "New York, New York."

She swayed from one side to the other as she sang the lyrics, tapping the cane in time to the music. About halfway through, she added a sashay from one side of the "stage" to the other, and finally, toward the end, finished up with chorus line kicks that were only about a quarter as high as those of the Radio City Music Hall Rockettes. It was a good thing she had the cane, since she was wheezing as she sang the last notes and lost her balance. Bernadine was only saved from an embarrassing—and possibly harmful—fall by smashing the cane on the floor and leaning on it.

There was polite applause as Ellison rushed in to make sure Bernadine didn't collapse. He helped her to a seat, then announced Willie and his magic. The former detective carried a small table to the front and performed a series of slight-of-hand tricks with more skill than Lilliana would have guessed he had. His smooth patter amused the audience as he did the tricks. At the end everyone was laughing, and he got a hearty round of applause.

Nancy had also decided to sing, and then Frank performed a juggling act. Ellison had been right; the residents were displaying talent Lilliana didn't know they had. She was truly enjoying herself—until Ellison stepped up to the mic again.

"And now, as our final performance, we have Lilliana Wentworth and Christopher MacAlistair singing a duet of 'If I Loved You' from *Carousel*."

Lilliana felt rooted to her spot; she was only able to move when Christopher cupped her elbow in his hand and said, "Let's go."

She'd never felt so nervous in her life as she did when she walked toward the front of the room. Rather than face the audience, she kept her eyes on Chris as he opened the bag and pulled out a Bose docking station into which his iPhone was already inserted. The retirement home didn't have a piano, and even if it had been possible for them to roll Christopher's over to the main building, there was no room in the television room for a baby grand. Instead, he'd recorded the piano accompaniment which they'd sing along to. Despite the fact they'd practiced the technique a dozen times or more, she was fearful she'd lose her way without the flexibility of Chris's live playing.

His eyes asked if she was ready. Hers said yes, even though she was afraid and shy at being the one to start. The same emotions as expressed in the song. Unsure, her voice wobbled a bit as she started the duet, then Christopher's strong baritone sang the second line and made her stronger, so that she sang the next line with assurance.

As their voices joined in harmony, all she was aware of was how beautiful they sounded as they blended, as if they were two parts of the same instrument, the lyrics echoing both the tentativeness and longing of their relationship. As they started the reprise, where he sang the lines she'd sung in the first rendition, he turned her with a gentle pressure so they were facing one another. Their eyes met, held, merged as their voices merged, until there was only Christopher there with her, only what she was feeling for him in her heart.

As the piano played the final arpeggio, she was startled by the burst of applause. She'd forgotten there was anyone else in the room.

Christopher gazed at her with a loving smile, dropped one of her hands so they could face the audience and take a bow as the applause thundered around them. Ellison was clapping the loudest as he stepped up to the mic.

"I don't think there's any doubt as to who our winners are." The clapping surged again, and he had to wait for it to subside before announcing, "First place goes to Lilliana Wentworth and Christopher MacAlistair." He handed a framed certificate to Christopher.

Lilliana didn't mind that there wasn't one for her. She'd already won her prize.

THANK YOU!

Thank you for reading *Royal Purple Murder!* I hope you enjoyed it. If you liked it, please consider leaving a review or rating on the site where it was purchased. Reviews on Goodreads are always appreciated. Your help in spreading the word is gratefully appreciated and reviews make a huge difference in helping new readers find the series.

Get your free bonus story!

See how Lilliana solves "The Case of the Silver Scorpion." You will also be notified of new releases, giveaways, and pre-release specials by signing up for my newsletter at https://elisemstone.com/newsletter/.

Books in the African Violet Club mystery series:

True Blue Murder
Blood Red Murder
Royal Purple Murder
Double Pink Murder
Ghost White Murder
Holly Green Murder

Books in the Community of Faith mystery series:

Faith, Hope, and Murder
Shadow of Death
A Game of Murder

If you like police procedurals, try my Lacy Davenport Mystery Shorts:

Murder at the Museum
Murder in Stella Mann

ABOUT THE AUTHOR

Elise M. Stone was born and raised in New York, went to college in Michigan, lived in the Boston area for eight years, and not too long ago moved to sunny Tucson, Arizona, where she doesn't have to shovel snow. Her first degree was in psychology, her second in computers. She's worked as a pizza maker, library clerk, waitress, social worker, programmer, and data jockey.

She wrote her first story in kindergarten. She loved writing stories. She wrote fewer and fewer stories through high school, finally abandoning the practice in college.

Every once in a while, she'd think wistfully of her dream to be a published author. "Royal Purple Murder" is her sixth published book.

I love hearing from readers. You can connect with me at:

Email: elisemstone@gmail.com
Twitter: @EliseMStone
Facebook: www.facebook.com/EliseMStone

ACKNOWLEDGMENTS

No one writes a book totally on their own. While I tend to be more independent than most, rarely showing my fiction to anyone until it's been through at least one complete revision, even I need another set of eyes to see things I miss.

For "Royal Purple Murder," Judith Ann Horner and Amelia Steiner provided those eyes. Each of them brought her own perspective to the work and helped me make this into a better story. They graciously volunteered their time and effort and willingly met my insane timetable.

The beautiful and perfectly appropriate new cover was designed by Susan Coils of Coverkicks. San took my vague ideas and turned them into an eye-catching design.

I also want to thank the Tucson Chapter of Sisters in Crime for their support and encouragement. Long before I felt worthy of calling myself a writer, they added "Author" to my membership badge and never doubted my abilities.

And last, but certainly not least, I'd like to thank all the people who have read my books. I have been overwhelmed at the response to the African Violet Club mystery series. When I started the first book as a lark during National Novel Writing Month, I never dreamed it would be published, much less enjoyed by so many people. Thank you not only for reading but for kindly leaving reviews of the books. I hope you enjoy

"Royal Purple Murder" as much as the previous novels.

Made in the USA
Las Vegas, NV
28 January 2022